A Bánh Mì for Two

TRINITY NGUYEN

Henry Holt and Company
New York

Henry Holt and Company, *Publishers since 1866*
Henry Holt® is a registered trademark of Macmillan Publishing Group, LLC
120 Broadway, New York, NY 10271 • fiercereads.com

Our books may be purchased in bulk for promotional, educational, or business use. Please
contact your local bookseller or the Macmillan Corporate and Premium Sales Department
at (800) 221-7945 ext. 5442 or by email at MacmillanSpecialMarkets@macmillan.com.

Library of Congress Cataloging-in-Publication Data is available.

First edition, 2024
Book design by Abby Granata
Printed in China.

ISBN 978-1-250-91082-0 (hardcover)
10 9 8 7 6 5 4 3 2 1

ISBN 978-1-250-91083-7 (paperback)
10 9 8 7 6 5 4 3 2 1

♡ ♡ ♡

To Vietnamese girls everywhere:
You are so loved.

Chapter One

LAN

Sài Gòn is a city whose humidity clings to the skin so sickly sweet that you wear its heat like clothes.

"Pfft," I snort. What a corny start. I delete the sentence.

Sài Gòn is a city where words and language float from stall to stall, person to person.

"Definitely corny," I say to myself, pressing backspace.

At the heart of this metropolis lies the sprawling hub of street food, finger-licking feasts prepared in front of the audience's eyes as they bask in the glorious aroma. If you walk through—

"Ughhhh." Groaning, I slam the laptop shut and bury my face in my palms without realizing how sticky they are from the plate of bánh cam I've been picking at. Now the sesame seeds that were all over my hands are all over my face instead—great. I stare at the untouched chè thái to my left, the floating jellies and cream glistening in the internet café's harsh lighting. It's sweating all over my notebook.

I sip on the chè, and its sweetness calms both the heat and my writer's block. Slowly, I open the laptop screen and peek at the document before sighing and holding down the delete key.

"What's wrong?" Triết asks, too busy clicking and clacking through a video game to even look. Sweat seeps through his T-shirt. "You've been hitting backspace on the same page for two hours now."

I scrunch my brows. "It hasn't been two hours. We just got here—"

The computer clock reads 16:00. *Shit.*

"You're right, for once," I say, to which he only shrugs before going back to yelling at his computer screen. "Maybe this is why I can't write. I'm distracted by your screaming match."

Triết shoots me an incredulous glance. "Whatever, you're just mad I'm about to be the best player in Asia. Meanwhile you barely have anything written."

I ignore the jab, choosing to grind through the jackfruit's crunchy texture instead. "Nothing is working. I tried writing at home but can't because it's home. I tried writing outside—which sounded like a good idea until I remembered it's too hot and you never know when dirt or sewer water is going to splash you in the face."

"So—excuses," he says.

"No." I roll my eyes. "I'm struggling with writer's block. It's a real thing."

Or at least that was what the internet told me when I resorted to Google-diagnosing the reasons why writing doesn't click for me anymore. All my words feel fake and blotchy, and street food feels less like an adventure and more like a chore now that I'm glued to a stall twenty-four seven, three sixty-five. Everything feels *wrong* now that Ba is gone.

I didn't spill my guts to Google, but the closest search result said writer's block, and so I had a name for this strange phenomenon. But it didn't really help: Writing has been more difficult since I self-diagnosed via the internet.

Triết huffs at the screen, his clicking becoming aggressively faster. "Who paired me up with the worst people in the server?"

It's often like this: me ranting about literally everything while my cousin pretends to listen—and sure, he does listen, but only to about one-third of what I say. "Remind me to never open up to you ever again." Still, I watch him take down another player before finding myself egging him on. "To your left! Triết, I said *left*. Hit E!"

"He's too tanky!"

"Hit E!" He does not, in fact, hit E. I shove his fingers off the keyboard and press the key myself, earning a screen that flashes *VICTORY!* before us. "Maybe I should call blogging quits and switch to esports."

"Um, please *don't*." He takes a bite of my jellies. "But okay, let's diagnose you. Maybe you can't write because you just can't. Take a walk? Clear your head?"

"You'd make an awful doctor." The embarrassing thing is, I've tried almost every tip the internet has to offer to combat writer's block, including listening to a ten-hour-long playlist of jazz music (which did not help).

He grins. "Good thing I'm not studying to be one."

"Maybe street food isn't my thing anymore." I fidget with the backspace key, feeling its comfort. Sometimes I wish I could just backspace parts of my life.

"I don't even know what I want to write about. I've talked so much about street food and where to find the best street food and what new street food to look out for, and I'm so, so sick of it."

"*You?* Sick of food? We're doomed." He winces at my light shoulder smack. "How about, maybe . . . try writing everything out, then editing it later?"

I blow at the strands in front of my face. "But write *what*? People want something new. I can't give them anything."

He hums before restarting the match, clicking through a new character avatar. "As your unofficial official social media manager, I'm here to tell you that people following your blog love the content you've been giving them. You don't have to do anything new. They keep asking

when you'll write something again. And I don't know much about blogging or writing, but I think they miss you."

My blog exists on both Instagram and its own website, but I put
the website on hiatus along with the longer blog posts last year. Now
all people get are pretty food photos in a curated feed paired with short
captions. Maybe that's all I'm meant to do, move on from the long think
pieces and rants I used to write, and just focus on the aesthetics. I wonder if people would care if I start featuring the work that I do as a bánh
mì seller on the blog—how would they react? It's not that I'm ashamed
of being a street food seller, it's just . . . what if they think I'm *uncool*?

How silly.

Sighing, I scroll through the comments on my Instagram, and for
every nice one, another question about my blogging hiatus follows.
"This writer's block and the pressure from my readers aren't helping. I
don't know if I could ever write something that they'll like again. What
if they hate my next blog post? Tear it apart?"

His gaze flickers to my laptop screen. "But why did you stop posting your food think pieces? You know that whatever you write, people
will still read it. It's been months."

A couple months seem so short compared to everything else, but
too much has changed. And I hate change.

"I got too busy." I shrug. "Speaking of which, we should head back."

He sighs, nodding and still not getting up. "Your mom will be fine.
There's fifteen minutes left, I could play another game and you could let
some more ideas stew. How does that sound?"

"No." The stall needs me—it's our family business—and it's what
good daughters are supposed to do, especially if their mother is a widow.

"Worth a shot." He shrugs and tells me to go first. I protest and
insist on splitting the bill, but Triết shoos me out the door anyway.

The bustling city greets me as I pass through the glass doors, and
at once, Sài Gòn overwhelms my senses. The noise of the streets. The

rich, decadent smells of phở and coffee. Humidity on my tongue. A light breeze down my back. The not-so-shy sun on my cheeks. People's voices from every direction, some haggling with shopkeepers and some gossiping about their in-laws. I don't see any familiar faces—I often don't—and I feel relieved. I can exist here in Sài Gòn, be just another part of this city.

But sometimes, I think about other cities. Are people lonely in Paris? Do they see faces they recognize on the subways in New York?

I scroll through my Instagram once again, analyzing every engagement. Every like and every comment—good or bad.

The flan here is THE BEST. Thank you, chị!

Best bánh xèo in Sài Gòn for sure.

Then there are the international comments.

Wishing I could visit!!!!!

Việt Nam is SO pretty!!!

I like each positive comment, replying *Thank you!* and *Thanks for reading!* under every single one. But sometimes I wonder if that's enough. What if one day I stop posting about food altogether? Or declare that I can't write anymore?

Will people even care? Or am I just colors and pixels on a screen, something people scroll past during their day? Flicking away a sesame seed on the screen, I'm about to close my phone when a notification chimes through. The username brings a smile to my face.

Evermore13: Love this post so much that I keep coming back to it! I miss your blogs, please write more soon.

Thank you, I type back to the one person who never fails to comment on all my posts—multiple times, too. *Please write more soon*: I zero in on those words. Maybe they're disappointed in me. They must be.

Running a street food stand is hard work. The only constant is yourself and the food you sell. My followers flock to every local business I showcase on Instagram, so even if my website is on hiatus, I still owe something to this community as a fellow street food seller. These aesthetic photos are more than my platform and followers. They've somehow helped the aunties and uncles out in the sun, allowing them to make a living.

Another notification pops up on my screen.

Evermore13: Putting this on your radar! Not just saying this because you're literally my favorite blogger, but I really think you could win.

My chest feels light at the words *favorite blogger*. Do I deserve that? I click on the link, which leads me to a site about a journalism contest. Chewing on my lips, I close the page and go to my website. I stare at my last post, written months ago: "Best Places to Hang Out After School." I remember perching around a plastic table surface, surrounded by friends, and suddenly, on this busy Sài Gòn street, loneliness hits me. Most of my classmates have left, pursuing passions and new lives all over the world while I'm . . . here. Just here.

An ache pounds at the base of my neck and I knead at it, accidentally plucking two strands of one black and one white hair in the process. It's not like I didn't want to leave. I had big dreams, too, once. But when death and grief change your life, then dreams become just that— dreams. Má can't tend the stall alone. This is a family business, and family means we do this *together*.

"Excuse me? Xin chào?" A gruff voice tugs at my attention, but also because the owner butchered the pronunciation.

"Hello, do you need help?" I take in the couple in front of me, two white tourists, each with their passport in one hand and suitcase in the other. They're wearing Patagonia sweatshirts—insanity in this heat— while carrying Herschel duffel bags at their sides.

Stunned, probably at my English, they motion me toward their phone, tapping furiously at a restaurant name. My heart flutters. They're on my Instagram. "Where. Is. This. Restaurant?" The man enunciates every word, dragging his vowels while his partner nods excitedly. My eyes almost roll out of their sockets.

"Cross the bridge after this street and turn right once you see a huge red pagoda." The actual directions are a lot more complicated than that, especially because the restaurant is tucked into an alleyway. But I'm sure they'll figure it out. There's a huge sign by the bridge.

"Thank you so much! One more question." He points to the lanterns floating above our heads, his face visibly confused. "Why does Việt Nam look like China? All these lanterns and pagodas . . . and even Chinese letters! What does this mean?"

Of course. I paste on the same smile I use every day at the bánh mì stall, and in my best customer service voice, I say: "Maybe try researching why when you're free." But I feel a twinge of guilt—they found this place on my Instagram—and backtrack. "Việt Nam has a lot of multi-ethnic communities. Not everywhere is just phở or bánh mì. We have immigrants here, too, and they've been flowing in and out for hundreds of years." And beyond all of that, Việt Nam's history and culture have been so deeply influenced by Chinese imperialism. Wait till these tourists realize *why* some of the architecture of Sài Gòn resembles Parisian homes.

"Thank you again." They both nod enthusiastically. "This is our first time in Asia and we've wanted to go to Sài Gòn for so long because of this blogger."

How nice that is, to pick a spot on the map and call it a vacation, or to have the money to pack all those suitcases and head for another country.

"The author is a genius for blogging in both Vietnamese and English, and they seem to know this city so well. Everything looks delicious, and I can't wait to try it all. Thank you for helping us." They nod at me and head for the bridge, their suitcases bouncing against the asphalt.

The blog was written in Vietnamese for the first year, but as I moved to advanced English in high school, I took up translating to practice, and so the Instagram captions are in both Vietnamese and English. Still, I wouldn't call myself a genius for having a bilingual blog.

It's not strange to see foreigners here. Maybe I should be proud that Sài Gòn is such a tourist destination. A must-see spot—a line other travel bloggers say often, but I've never understood it. My city isn't a must-see spot, it's what I'm used to. *My home.* All the other travel blogs portray Sài Gòn as this glamorous city where young people can find themselves and live their best lives. I can't do that. My life isn't glamorous. It's a cycle of work and bánh mì crumbs and even more work.

But readers don't want to see that; they want an escape, something beautiful. The blog used to be a way to capture a portrait of my home, but now every follower feels like more pressure to help turn Sài Gòn into a tourist playground.

Just as I near the bánh mì stall, my phone chimes again.

Evermore13: I'm on my way to Sài Gòn right now and can't wait to try all your yummy spots! <3

Chapter Two

VIVI

Faking a trip is a lot harder than I imagined, especially if it includes lying to your immigrant parents.

"Are you sure I can't just text my mom now?" I chew on my lower lip as my eyes follow the chaos unfolding on the plane: people shuffling, flight attendants asking us to be patient, and of course, babies crying. The same babies that have been wailing for the entire eighteen-hour flight. I get why my parents are so travel averse.

Cindy rolls her eyes at me. "Singapore is sixteen hours ahead of California. We told your mom that we'd land at six. It's only five."

"It's only an hour ahead—"

My best friend opens the twenty-page outline that we wrote in excruciating detail about our Fake Study Abroad Trip. "We said that we're on Singapore Airlines flight 2044, which hasn't even landed yet. Knowing your mom, she's probably up watching the flight tracker right now."

I snort. "She was so scared we'd crash into the ocean."

"Well, that turbulence was no joke." She shudders. "I really thought she jinxed us."

"My mom thinks the entire world is out to get us." After living in Orange County, California, all my life with parents who'd rather spend every day staring at the same palm trees outside our windows, the plane ride was more thrilling than scary. "The jello theory explains that we technically can't go down during turbulence."

"*Technically*," she repeats. "Well, it's not Singapore . . . but hey, we're finally in Việt Nam."

"I know. I can't believe it. This place is *real* and not just photographs or Google images." There's an uneasiness in my stomach, but that's probably because I'm lying to everyone I know back home.

I look out the plane window, and my heart flutters at the cityscape beyond the tall trees. I'm really here.

Unlike other Vietnamese families, mine doesn't go on annual vacations to the "homeland." Weekly gatherings at mom-and-pop phở shops in Little Saigon are the closest I've ever gotten to the real deal. Every Sunday, family friends would share stories about Việt Nam, about mouth-watering food and expansive landscapes and bustling streets. I envied them. I asked my parents over and over why we couldn't visit, but they always said, *You're too young to understand*. It made no sense.

But now I'm finally here, in the homeland I've wanted to visit all my life. I scroll through photos and screenshots in my phone, trying to remember everything I want to experience here. Fresh coffee every morning at a local café, watching the sun peek over the horizon as the city wakes. Meals eaten while squatting on kiddie stools on the side of the road as the smell of street food seeps into my clothes. My thumb pauses on a screenshot of a blog post, "Best Places to Hang Out After School." Maybe—like once in a lifetime maybe—I'll meet the person behind the Blog and thank them for bringing me here. Or maybe not, because that'd be a little weird.

Who knows.

Cindy taps on my shoulder impatiently. "Hurry, I need to pee."

We scramble out of our seats and down the aisle. My carry-on is absurdly heavy, and I groan, thinking about Mom's antics. "My suitcase is going to explode from all the vitamin supplements my mom *insisted* I take for extra immune system support. She said, and I quote, 'You won't know what kinds of sickness you'll catch abroad.'" Maybe it's an immigrant-parent thing to always be extra, extra careful.

"On the bright side, you've brought the entire CVS store with us!"

"True. Need melatonin or super-fast-acting flu medicine? It's on me—"

I'm barely finishing my sentence when someone plows right into me, sending my purse into the air. My eyes widen in shock as we watch it fly up and land with a thud that knocks all its contents onto the floor.

Photographs of strangers stare up at me. Well, not strangers—they're family. At least, I *think* they're family. It's not like I can ask Mom, who I stole these photos from. She'd just reprimand me for going through her things, and still wouldn't give me any answers.

I pick up each photo, smoothing out their vintage edges before tucking them safely back into my purse. The photo of Mom in a pretty áo dài in front of a cathedral I insert into my wallet instead.

"You okay?" Cindy picks up the last photo from the ground—three women smiling in front of a tall building, maybe a marketplace. One *definitely* is Mom, while the others share the same nose. "Already getting into your first accident abroad. Guess that trip insurance was worth it."

I place the photograph in the same pocket as Mom's photo. "I've stared at these black-and-white faces so much, spent so much time imagining how they'll act and what they'll say to me . . . I can't believe they're real people, and I'm potentially meeting them soon."

"*Potentially meeting?* Vivi, we didn't just fly across the globe for you to hallucinate this meeting in your head. We'll find your mom's family *and* find out why your parents never wanted to take you here."

I gulp. "I guess. Where do we even start? I have no address. No names. And my mom would rather put me on the first flight home than ever tell me."

Her gaze softens. "We'll figure it out. This city can't be *that* big. We'll find someone."

But as we both stare at Sài Gòn through the airport windows, we know there's a very slim chance of finding my mom's family. The city *is* that big.

Most Vietnamese kids in the States grow up speaking to their families in Việt Nam through phone or video calls. Not me. Mom and Dad keep that part of our lives separate like a scar they want hidden.

Not that Dad can really do much; his parents died when he was super young. The only things I really know about my grandparents are that my grandma passed sometime during the war while my grandpa and Dad became refugees when Dad was three. Grandpa didn't make it to Dad's wedding. So Dad grew up with all things American: burger joints and Happy Meals, the twenty-six letter alphabet that doesn't contain Vietnamese diacritics, and football (the man really loves football, although I can't understand why).

Mom, on the other hand . . . I know we still have family here. I've seen her taping boxes to be mailed to Việt Nam. Still, she's never shared much, and the place across the Pacific Ocean remained an enigma throughout my childhood.

Mom accidentally reverse psychology'd me, and her refusal to talk about Sài Gòn only made me more curious. When I first googled Việt Nam, textbook images of decapitated bodies scarred me. I grew up thinking Việt Nam looked like rural land where everyone treks ten miles to school. This airport—city—does not look rural. At all.

"What's the first thing we should do in Sài Gòn?" Cindy huffs beside me, walking too fast for both our short legs.

"Nap? Eat? For you, pee."

She rolls her eyes. "What did that blogger you've been following for years say? What's the name again . . . A Bánh Mì something?"

"*A Bánh Mì for Two*," I say immediately.

"Right." She nods slowly, raising an eyebrow. "Any tourist recommendations? You've read like every single post almost a bazillion times, probably memorized the entire blog by now."

"They don't do posts like that. Everything is focused on local life. Hidden gems, that sort of stuff."

I ran into *A Bánh Mì for Two* while looking up Vietnamese food history for a paper one night. The first post I read described how phở is actually a product of French colonialism in so much detail that I ended up citing the entire blog. I stayed up all night scouring the site. The words made me feel warm, comforted. I hadn't realized what Việt Nam is actually like.

I scroll through *A Bánh Mì for Two*'s Instagram every day, hope in my chest that the blog's hiatus will end soon. I miss their writing, and I miss imagining myself in their words even more.

We hurry through the terminal to baggage claim, the coolness of the airport replaced by the city's thick humidity and sweltering heat. A sign hangs above us: WELCOME TO THÀNH PHỐ HỒ CHÍ MINH. So many bodies trickling in and out. A sense of nostalgia washes over me. Home but not home. Scents I've always known, and a language spoken throughout Little Saigon, and yet it's the first time I'm here. Sure, I look Vietnamese, and I can somewhat speak Vietnamese, although I'm not really fluent. I feel like I'm not Vietnamese enough, but I'm not American enough, either. Unlike other students in the program, I can't just pass as a foreigner, but I can't blend in with the locals, either. It's a constant tug-of-war within me: being Vietnamese, but not really . . . and being American, but not really. Will I fit in—ever?

Cindy came up with the plan to study abroad for our first semester of college, and I signed on without a second thought. Why should we be stuck in smelly dorm rooms and share gross showers with people when we can do the same but *abroad*.

Still, I'm not where I'm supposed to be. Guilt eats at me for lying. Taking advantage of my parents' trust did not feel good. But my parents didn't pry. They never do. They've always silently signed whatever academic forms I needed them to. I picked AP classes and submitted college applications on my own, skills I've learned from being a daughter of immigrants and the first of my family to go to college.

I breathe in the smell of motorcycle fumes and diesel from nearby cars. It's evening and the sun is still scorching hot, baking us all in her ruthless heat.

Cindy mirrors my action, wrinkling her nose. "Ew."

"My mom said that when she first landed at LAX, she breathed in the scents of LA and knew she had found freedom. So, I wanted to try it here," I say sheepishly.

"Freedom must have smelled like piss and pollution, then." She throws her head back laughing.

Now it's my turn to roll my eyes.

My parents talk a lot about America being the land of opportunity, and they're always going on about freedom and liberty. But as I watch them struggle with the language barrier and find menial work that requires them to rise at 5:00 a.m. and toil until after sunset, I wonder if they meant the land of *missed* opportunities.

Mom refuses to speak about her life before the States and why she chose such a life of hardship over Việt Nam. *I did all of this for you, you know.* Việt Nam is always spoken of as a reminder that I shouldn't take things for granted. That I have it better, that I should be grateful. That I shouldn't wonder why or want to look back.

Maybe I wasn't raised right because I've always wanted to look back, to look across the Pacific and imagine our lives within the winding shape of Việt Nam. With another deep inhale of Sài Gòn's fumes, I ready myself as we step into the cab taking us to the dormitory and to the heart of the city. My parents' home.

The very place I've daydreamed of since stumbling upon *A Bánh Mì for Two*.

Chapter Three

LAN

—

Bánh mì fuels Sài Gòn, from the livelihoods of us vendors to the people we feed. I tie the makeshift plastic cover over the stall, wrangling the strings while the wheels groan. I win the tug-of-war and dust off the bánh mì crumbs stuck to my jeans. The sun paints streaks of orange and red throughout the sky, signaling the end of a long day. A damp towel meets my forehead, halting the incoming heatstroke as I shuffle through extra bills and stuff them into my pocket. Muscle memory moves my body, a monotonous dance I've learned as a street food seller. After spending all day with sweat on my face, I'd rather nap than write.

This writer's block doesn't seem to be going away anytime soon.

"Cảm ơn, chị!" a student thanks me as I hand her the order.

"Enjoy. Come back soon!" I say the phrase I've practiced in the mirror way too many times. Our mood sells food. No matter the type of day I have, a smile must always be on my face.

I watch the student's white áo dài flutter as she walks. Nestled in the heart of Sài Gòn, our business depends on restless and hungry students. They drive by on their motorbikes every morning, throwing bills for a bánh mì ốp la before hurrying off to class. A pang of regret pinches in the base of my throat, and I turn my attention back to flicking baguette pieces off my pants. Sometimes I wish I could scrub all the crumbs off my body, emerging as a clean slate without smelling like a bakery.

"Lan!" Má calls from the opposite side of the street, bags and bags of bánh mì ingredients in her arms. "Come help!"

"Why did you go without me!" I shout back as I cross to help her. "Your back and shoulders are going to hurt from carrying all of this."

"Don't yell at your mother." She clicks her tongue but hands me the bags anyway. "I'm still strong."

We cross back, Má stumbling slightly as she fishes for the painkillers. I look away, swallowing hard.

Chronic pain that started after Ba's passing. She hid it from me for a long time, even after she'd gotten her diagnosis and told everyone else we know. Our relationship has always been distant, with me attached to Ba's hip when he was still with us. Although we spend more hours together than not, Má seems to confide in anyone but me.

"What's with all the ingredients? We're closed for the day."

Má jerks her head at the building across the street. "Special order. Bà Hai asked us to make bánh mì for their new international students. It's mostly simple since foreigners can be kind of picky."

Picky is an understatement. "I still remember when a group of tourists asked us if the patê was sanitary." Little did they know that *patê* isn't even a Vietnamese word. They wouldn't be asking these questions if they were in France.

"People are a bit curious," Má says, occupying the space next to me and undoing all my hard work of tidying up the stall.

"They shouldn't ask us stupid questions, though. I can't count how many times someone made a face walking by the snail lady next door.

What's wrong with eating snails?" I continue, helping her unpack the ingredients.

She passes me a baguette. I lather the bread with patê before pressing grilled meat inside the loaf, finishing it with pickled vegetables and a light drizzle of soy sauce. Maybe this bánh mì with too much patê will be for someone who's *curious.*

"Con ơi, there's only so much we can do," Má says, resigned. "What use does complaining do for us? We can just work and hope that's enough."

With a tight lip, I nod my head. "Yes, Má."

"What's going on here?" Triết returns from "studying" at the internet café. I think he's hardly studying rather than studying hard.

"Special order," I call back. "You're helping or not?"

He's definitely rolling his eyes at me. "Geez, I'm here."

"Lan." Má places a hand on my shoulders. I flinch instinctively, my stomach dropping when I see her concerned face. "Why don't you take off early? Triết can help me."

"What about you?" I don't like the thought of Má being alone.

"I'll be fine!" She waves me off. "Triết is just as fast as you."

"But—"

"I'm offended, Lan. You're implying that I can't take care of my favorite aunt in the entire world," Triết butts in. I open my mouth to retort, but he ushers me away. "It's okay, I'll be here with her. I promise," he whispers, handing me my tote bag and ruffling my hair before taking his post next to Má. He has a towering figure—protective and almost like Ba's.

After Ba, Triết filled the hole in our lives. Maybe it's his nonchalant personality or the way that he takes after Ba, but Má's sullen expressions cracked after he came to live with us. She laughs more and even cooks more. Still, jealousy tugs at me for not being the person that pulled Má out from grief.

"Stop it, Cindy!" a voice squeaks from across the street.

They must be the international students, judging from the way they're gawking at the city. A Vietnamese girl stands out from the group, though I can tell she's American based on her accent. Overseas Vietnamese come all the time, always trickling into the city either because of nostalgia and a filial duty to visit, or simply because they want to strut the streets with accents and designer clothes. They're not hard to spot. Like Má says, Vietnamese recognizes Vietnamese.

I tear my gaze from the students, but not before catching the girl's eyes on me, too. *Maybe she's curious*, Má's words echo in my head.

Well, at least her curiosity led her somewhere. My curiosity could hardly afford a flight outside of Việt Nam.

With one look back at the stall, I slip into the maze of streets. Navigating Sài Gòn thrills me. My body twists and turns through the motorbikes, each step almost like a dance. Lanterns line the streets as the city readies itself for Tết Trung Thu, the Mid-Autumn Festival. A goldfish lantern glimmers on the side of a shop, its holographic scales reflecting the evening sun. Grief creeps up my spine. Chinatown lion dancing. Me on Ba's shoulders, reaching for the sky and the lanterns above us.

Another Trung Thu without him.

Instead of hurrying home, my feet take me to the nearby park as I spy the sunset and its red hues looming over the Sài Gòn skyline. I watch kids flying their kites nearby, some riding bikes with kites strapped to their backs. I make my way toward the street food vendors, settling on cá viên chiên before sliding onto a blue plastic stool and feeling lonelier than usual.

The worker slides a piping-hot plate of fish balls onto my tiny table. I snap photos of the plate from different angles, rearranging the brown, white, and orange fish balls for maximum effect. After almost a hundred photos, I pick the picture of me holding the plate against the pink sunset, editing its saturation and vibrancy before tapping share on Instagram.

I open my phone and stare at the submission announcement again. Instead of sleeping last night, my head swam through different ideas. Maybe a story about the lemon trees by the Amalfi Coast. The grand Angkor Wat in Siem Reap. Or even California, where most Vietnamese Americans are, with the ocean at their doorstep and—well, I don't know what else. 'Cause I've never been.

The submission requirement is one story, one piece with the following theme: The Most Beautiful City in the World. The grand prize is a feature on the *Southeast Asia Travel Magazine* website and a grant that would keep our business afloat for at least a year. Má wouldn't have to take special orders late in the day anymore, and maybe we could close early some days, too.

If Ba was still with us, would he encourage me to enter—to write? Would he believe in me?

Ba, I miss you.

I let the thought sink in, allowing it to course through my mind for the first time in months. When you miss someone, you want to be with them. But no flights can take me to him.

My feet carry me to the edge of the park, where the synthetic grass meets the river. I pick up a rock and release it from my hand, watching it bounce atop the murky water before sinking, invisible beneath the lotuses.

The day's heat is simmering down as the sun starts to sink below the Sài Gòn skyline. Swirling the straw around inside the coconut with one hand, I click my pen with the other and begin to write, all while the Vietnamese American girl's face floats into my head. I wonder why she's here, and why so many people come to this city.

But that's not my business.

Chapter Four

VIVI

I'm not used to being around this many people. And I've definitely never been around this many people that look like *me*.

Living in Little Saigon was almost like living in a bubble—Vietnamese spoken at every turn, Vietnamese mom-and-pop shops at every corner, and Vietnamese kids being the majority at the local high schools. Still, my little bubble can't compare to the enormousness of Sài Gòn.

People speed by on motorbikes, grunting over potholes. They laugh with friends at food stalls and dodge traffic like experts. A whole new world I've never known, never grew up with. It's overwhelming, but I'm so glad I'm here.

I chew on the twenty-hour-old bánh bao that Mom packed for me. She ran out early yesterday morning just to get me my favorite food before my flight. But the bao tastes like rubber—too cold, too stale—and not the same as when she'd make them every Friday with pork, spices, Chinese sausage, and quail eggs.

I wonder if Mom knows the best bánh bao spots in Sài Gòn; if she even remembers. It's hard to imagine Mom as the girl in the photos buried inside her closet, smiling beneath the same Việt Nam sun as me. I haven't ever seen her smile like that before. Whoever this girl is can't be Mom.

Yet her name is on the back of the photo, next to the date when it was taken.

"Vivi! Will you quit staring and finally help me unload your suitcases? You're right. Your parents did pack a truckload of crap—"

"Cindy!" I hush her. She gives me a "what the hell" face. "Don't air out my dirty laundry to everyone." My voice low, almost whisper-yelling.

Cindy, unlike me, still speaks at a normal volume. "Are you embarrassed? Why? It's a suitcase. For packing stuff. That you packed." She says it so matter-of-factly that I almost convince myself I'm the one being unreasonable.

"We're trying to impress people here." I help her drag my *definitely*, very, awfully heavy suitcase. "And I want to be, I don't know, cool? This isn't high school. These people have no idea who we are. It's like a clean slate."

"Fine." She rolls her eyes. "Then can I have a new personality, too? Oh! What if we invent alter egos for ourselves abroad?"

"You sound like a sexpat. What's next? We have affairs abroad and never tell our families about it?" I never would have learned the word *sexpat* if not for *A Bánh Mì for Two*. One of the older blog posts on the website, "Ten Reasons to Never Travel to Việt Nam," mocks the types of Westerners who come and "colonize brides." It's one of their least popular posts and received so many hateful comments that the author locked the comment thread. The post remains on the site to this day. I never understood the criticisms from readers. The author wrote about their experience in their home country. I mean, *I* definitely wouldn't try to butt into the conversation since I know absolutely nothing about Việt Nam.

Cindy winces at my suggestion. "No, thanks. We're not even rich enough to be sexpats. I do not have enough money to fund a green card for my foreign spouse."

I click my tongue. "What alter egos should we try, then?"

"We can pretend to be enemies."

"Nope. You're going to cry the moment you try being mean to me. It's impossible for you."

"You're right," she sighs. "I guess we'll just be Cindy Rodriguez and Vivi Huỳnh. True to ourselves."

"You're so dramatic."

"Says you."

The street outside our dormitory, thankfully, isn't as busy as the city center. People walk back and forth with ease, some carrying buckets atop their heads while others engage in screaming matches across the street. My eyes dart everywhere, studying every corner and every small shop, landing on a girl staring straight at us. Tanned skin with a posture that screams confidence. She looks like she belongs, like she knows this city. Our gaze meets for a fleeting second before she immediately turns away, her braid dancing by her side. Embarrassed, I turn away, too.

Was she judging us—judging me? Did she know that I'm not like her? That I'm Vietnamese but not from–Việt-Nam Vietnamese?

A clap reverberates through the air. "Everyone! Welcome to your home for the next four months." Anh Huy, our program chaperone and instructor, unlocks the tall doors to the dormitory. He eases us in, taking our luggage and paying special close attention to mine. "This is quite heavy, Vivi."

Oh my God.

One by one, we manage to drag ourselves through the door and into the common room, sleep in our eyes while we take turns complaining about how sore and tired each of us are. My poor back especially, after an out-of-control toddler kept kicking at it the entire plane ride. I'm about to fall asleep right then and there, until the sweet scent of grilled meat overwhelms my nose.

"It smells like thịt nướng." I'd know that smell anywhere, especially because it's my parents' favorite thing to do on the weekends: flipping skewers by the banana tree in our backyard. Maybe it reminds them of Việt Nam.

An elderly lady carrying a full plate of bánh mì saunters through a partition, and my eyes bulge at the feast between her arms. Bánh mì. Tons of bánh mì. "Xin chào! Welcome! You must all be so tired from your trips. I am Bà Hai, the residential coordinator of this dorm. Here, have some." She shoves loaves cut in half into our hands.

"You must be người mỹ gốc việt." She studies my face. My stomach flips. Of course she knows I'm Vietnamese American—this is a study abroad program for Americans, after all—but will I ever just look Vietnamese? "Do you like patê?"

"My favorite." Who *doesn't* like patê?

"Good." She smiles bashfully. "You get the bánh mì with the most patê."

"Thank you, Bà," I say, not forgetting to bow. Cindy follows suit while the other students awkwardly copy me.

Taking my first bite of Vietnamese food in Sài Gòn, I chew through the umami explosion on my tongue. The tender meat melts like butter, the patê mixing with its rich, fatty taste. Baguette crumbs decorate my mouth and I lick my lips, savoring each flake. My taste buds meet the pickled vegetables next, the flavor not too sweet or sour, as if each ingredient down to the soy sauce was prepared with care.

Cindy smacks her lips beside me. "First meal abroad and it didn't disappoint. Maybe I can live here forever."

Bà Hai cackles, motioning us for seconds. "I knew it was the right call to get bánh mì! Did you see the stall right across the street? Bánh Mì 98 is the best in the city."

My new roommate and a Vietnamese local, Nga, takes a suitcase and guides me to our room. I drag my other luggage up through the narrow, spiraling staircases, pausing to pant when we unlock the door. Việt Nam is *really* working out my legs so far.

Nga gives me the spare key. "Make yourself at home! I cracked the window open, but you can close it if you want."

I step into our small but cozy room. It has two beds, one in each corner, and two desks. A typical dorm room experience. Our window stares out onto the streets, offering a view of Sài Gòn with its colorful buildings, pagodas, and skyscrapers. I feel so small, like a droplet in this vast city. The sun glows as people hustle back and forth in the streets, most wearing some kind of hat to shield themselves from the heat. Not bothering to unpack my suitcase, I jump right into bed and sink into the wonderfully soft mattress. Drowsiness tugs at my eyelids and I allow it.

The alarm titled TEXT MOM goes off and I send her a quick message promising I'm safe along with a curated selfie Cindy took of me against the airport wall—no Sài Gòn cityscape in the background. She responds with a thumbs-up emoji right away. It's almost 4:00 a.m. in California.

I think about the future Vivi in four months. Will I be a different person in December? Will this trip change how I see my parents? How will I see Mom, after learning about the life she had here?

Will I finally know why Mom was so happy here? Why she left?

My phone chimes.

Mom: Mommy thương con. Stay safe. Don't talk to strangers.

Chapter Five

LAN

Exactly twenty-six pages of garbage. Words don't flow out of my pen like they used to, and the more I stare at the scribblings inked throughout my notebook, the more it makes me nauseous. The sun has set, the velvet blue sky draping itself over Sài Gòn. In the distance, Landmark 81 looms over the city. Students are probably trickling into parks and businesses, gossiping over drinks and food. People are dressing up for date nights or visiting District 1's sprawling new-age boutiques, restaurants, and bars. Maybe I would be joining them if Ba were still alive. Maybe I'd be in a karaoke room right now, debating over songs to sing with new friends.

But I can't.

Time to go home.

I retrace my steps back from the park, looping through alleyways as the familiar sight of monsoon-weathered walls and colorful homes comes into view.

"Lan! How was work today?" Dì Sáu, the flan lady, spots me while tidying up her street food stall at the corner of our alley: a cart for the flan, coolers for the ice, and plastic utensils for customers. She sets up the stall right in front of her house, hauling fresh and homemade dessert out every hour of the day.

I rush over and help stack the plastic stools. "Today was fine. We didn't have to stay too late. I even got to go to the park and get some fish balls!"

She clicks her tongue. "You always work so hard. Even helping me clean up. I've been able to close early, too. New customers came like flies, telling me someone recommended this place! What nonsense, no one knows about this tiny alley. But whoever it is, I hope they get good karma."

The left corner of my mouth curves upward. "I'm sure they'll be happy to know they've helped you."

"How have you been? And your mom?" she asks, concern in her eyes.

I've anticipated this question. Everyone asks me how I'm doing every chance they get, as if I can't handle things on my own. "We're doing good. Don't worry about us." I smile, making sure to flash my teeth to amp the persuasion.

"Tsk." She clicks her tongue. "You shouldn't be like me, all haggard under the heat every day. You should be out with friends, going to university, enjoying your youth."

Not knowing what else to say, I plant my eyes on the leather part of my sandals. "I'm okay, Dì. Going out and stuff isn't my thing."

Who knows? I haven't been out with friends in so long. Street food dates are more or less a blur in my memories.

She slumps her shoulders, reaching for my hand. "Let yourself breathe sometimes, Lan."

But I can't afford to, I want to say.

"Go home. I can do the rest myself. Remember to eat lots and take care of yourself, okay?" She plops a plastic cup of sweet yellow flan into my hand.

"I will. Thank you, Dì."

Vietnamese is a funny language. Dì, chị, bà, and other honorifics all literally mean auntie sister, and grandma, yet we still address other people not related by blood with these words. Related or not, we're connected by bonds stronger than familial ones.

Even in a city as big as Sài Gòn, everyone just knows each other somehow. Someone you haven't heard of? They're probably someone's teacher's mother's cousin. Or maybe a friend of a friend of a friend.

The mango tree comes into view as my feet carry me toward the one-story house I call home. Ba's orchids greet me as I walk through the gates, shades of purple, pink, and yellow shining against the gloomy gray of our house.

Triết greets me with an absent-minded wave, his eyes glued to the TV he brought home one day.

"You're back? Công viên again? Shame on you if you didn't bring any food home."

"Just because you're so mean, all the cá viên chiên is mine."

He finally tears his gaze away from the TV at my comment. "Hey! I made canh khổ qua for you! Don't eat all of the fish balls. You know they're my favorite."

Classic Triết, always demanding. But I can't stay mad at him when he does my chores without asking for much in return. There's a shared understanding between us, especially after Má's diagnosis.

Má parts the curtains from her sewing room, kissing me on the cheek and grabbing a bowl from the drying rack. "Scoop me some rice. I'll eat with you."

"You didn't have dinner yet?" I ask, worry in my voice. It's already past dinnertime and her abdominal pain gets worse if she doesn't eat on time.

"I wanted to eat with you. You took too long to get back."

Guilt sours my tongue, and suddenly, the soup becomes overpoweringly bitter in my mouth. "I'm sorry, I'll come straight home next time."

"No, I meant that you were missing out on Triết's food. I just wanted to try it with you, in case he poisons me," she teases. He sticks his tongue out at her.

I laugh. "I'll kick him out and send his butt straight back to Bến Tre."

Triết, still chewing, pulls the chopsticks from his mouth and shakes them at me. "Don't you dare." He waves me off and goes back to watching soccer, yelling some sports nonsense at the TV.

Má sets a plate of cá kho tộ on the table, and pours some nước mắm into a small dish next to it, adding Thai chilies and a squeeze of lime. It's hard to find a Vietnamese person who doesn't like fish sauce. There's probably more fish sauce in our bodies than blood.

Ba, more than anyone, drank nước mắm like water. It's been four years since he passed, and yet I still catch glimpses of him in everything. From the sky to nước mắm, as well as every mundane thing in the world—it all doesn't feel the same without Ba.

"What did you do today? After work?" Má asks.

"Nothing, Má. I just went to the park and, um, tried to write." Maybe she's upset at me for leaving early. I should have stayed at the stall. "From now on, I won't leave—"

"Write!" She beams, slamming her chopsticks on the table before clutching my hand, startling me. "I didn't know you're still writing."

I'm not. "Um, yeah. Just some scribbling. Nothing much."

"That's good." She nods, eyes creased in the corner. I'm suddenly transported back to when Ba was here with us, right in this kitchen, when Má heard about our silly idea of a blog project and smiled so bright. "You've always been a talented writer. Just like your dad."

I prepare for the gloom of grief to come over Má's face, but nothing happens. There's a slight grin on her lips.

"And don't worry about the stall or me. Things will be fine. Just continue writing, I know that's what makes you happy."

I only nod.

Wait. Writing. My notebook.

"I think I left my notebook at the park." I jolt from the table, almost flipping over the plates.

"Are you sure?" Má asks, her eyebrows scrunched. It's late, con. Maybe you misplaced it somewhere."

I dig into my tote bag, dumping everything out but the notebook. "Yes. I have to go back."

"We can get you a new one tomorrow," Triết chimes in. "It's dark, so who knows if you'll find it."

My stomach drops at the thought. "No, it's . . ." The notebook Ba gifted me for my twelfth birthday. I decided today of all days to use it in hopes that the feel of fresh paper would help me write. "I'll be back soon!"

How on earth could I forget? Today is not my day. As my feet power through the streets, I pray to the stars and whatever good karma Dì Ba sent me that the notebook will still be there. I don't care about the twenty-six pages of garbage I've written, but it's one of my last connections to Ba. I can't lose it, too.

Please, whoever and whatever you are, please send something good my way.

Chapter Six

VIVI

Custard pudding. Salty and buttery puffs. Lạp xưởng sticky rice. Mung bean pancakes. On days when I'm sick, pork floss served on piping-hot congee sprinkled with black pepper and dried onions. Flavors so distinct I see the food even with my eyes closed. Textures that shaped so much of my childhood.

A pillow lands squarely on my face.

"Ewwwwww, Viv! You're salivating all over the bed!" Cindy's voice echoes through the room, its shrill pitch hauling me from my sleep.

I muffle my face with the pillow and pretend to drown her out. "For the love of God, let me sleep. You passed out on that plane. Not me."

She yanks the pillow from underneath my arms and smacks my face with it—hard. "You slept for two hours. That's enough rest already. We're going to dinner. Our first dinner in Việt Nam!" She shakes my shoulders. "I'm going to jump on you."

I refuse to budge.

"One."

"Cindyyyyyyyyyyyyy . . ."

"Two."

"I would never do this to you."

"Three!" she yelps, her voice somehow squeakier, and clamors onto my twin XL, which was definitely not made for pillow fights. Cindy jabs at my sides, tickling me.

"Okay okay okay! I'll go!" This girl is relentless. "I *said* I'll go!"

"Get up by yourself right now and prove it."

I whine into the pillows. "Why now? We have months to see Sài Gòn!"

Cindy huffs. "You're the only Vietnamese American in the program, so you're obligated to be the most excited."

A knock comes from the other side of the door. "Hurry up! We're hungry!" Nga calls out.

"Coming!" I yell back. Shit, everyone's first impression of me is ruined because of one tiny nap. *Sleepyhead* is basically branded on my forehead now.

I stick out my tongue at Cindy, who's raising one eyebrow with a very, very smug smile. "Give me exactly three minutes to wash my face. And yes, time me," I dare her.

I race down our tiny hallway and splash water onto my face before lathering on deodorant and stumbling down the stairs. The rest of the cohort is lounging in the living room, debating where to eat. They wave me in, and my ears perk up at the mention of ốc xào—chewy snails drowned in an explosion of spices, Thai basil, and lemongrass. Mom makes this dish often, and a wave of homesickness slams into me. I miss her, and I wish I could text her about my flight, about the bánh mì we ate, and everything about this city.

Together, we strap on our sandals and wander through the streets. As much as delicious fatty sea snails enthrall us, so does Sài Gòn's night-life. It's electrifying and dizzying in the best ways.

"Damn, Viv," Cindy says. "Your favorite blog didn't lie about Sài Gòn."

Nga glances back at us. "What travel blogs do you read?"

My ears feel hot. I wasn't expecting to be put on the spot about blogging and Instagram and well, my somewhat parasocial relationship to this stranger. "Um, I only follow *A Bánh Mì for Two.*"

Nga jumps, turning to me, her eyes wide. "I know *A Bánh Mì for Two!* That blog is huge here. A lot of kids our age read it, and the businesses they post about get hundreds more customers the next morning."

No way. After years of pestering Cindy about the blog, it feels great to know that people in Sài Gòn love *A Bánh Mì for Two* as much as I do.

"I like that the author writes about food. I mean, what's not to like about food? Their blogs about friendship over cà phê sữa đá and spring roll–making parties on weekends made me want my own big friend group, too," I say. "And to be honest, everything about that blog made me want to come to Việt Nam. Now I'm here."

"Soooo poetic and romantic," Cindy comments.

Nga pulls out her phone and scrolls down *A Bánh Mì for Two*'s Instagram feed. "We should definitely visit this cá viên chiên place they literally just posted about. It's at the same park we're heading to!"

My heart races. The same park? I'm surprised Nga's even more on top of *A Bánh Mì for Two*'s notifications than I am. "Maybe . . . the blogger will still be there? We can look for—oomf."

My nose lands right in the middle of someone's solid back.

"Maybe look where you're going instead," Cindy teases. "Man, you have such a crush on that blogger."

"Cindy!" I say, my jaw hanging open. "It's not a crush—"

"Then a weird parasocial relationship."

I roll my eyes. "Fine. You can call it that. Wait, why are we stopping?"

She shrugs, standing on tiptoes to see over the rest of the group.

"We're about to cross the street to the park," Nga says.

Minh, the other Vietnamese local student volunteer in the program, extends his arm toward a busy traffic-filled street. "All right, kids, lesson number one: Learn how to cross without stoplights."

A student gapes at Minh. "You're kidding."

Thank goodness we paid for travel insurance.

Motorbikes, cars, and bicycles swarm the street. None of them look like they'll be stopping anytime soon, but pedestrians around us just jump straight into the fray. Like they're following some unspoken rule, the cars and pedestrians weave around each other. No one slows down, but somehow, no one crashes. I wipe my sweaty palms on my pants and grab Cindy's hand.

Nga laughs at us. "Americans. Just follow me."

Cindy looks at me with alarm and I almost burst out laughing. People jaywalk in the States all the time, but *this* is another beast. People on motorbikes swerve by the group, blaring their horns and shouting in Vietnamese.

We all let out a collective breath once we've crossed.

"That wasn't so bad?" I nudge Cindy.

She looks at me like I've grown another head. "You do it alone next time, then."

"Maybe not."

We walk over to the ốc xào vendor next to the river and pull three plastic tables together, wide and large enough to fit everyone. One by one, we sit on the tiny stools. The evening breeze teases my back and takes the humid air and sweat with it.

Nga comes back with bottles of beer, setting one in front of each person. "Listen and learn! This is how Vietnamese people nhậu. *Nhậu* just means drinking beer and eating food—such a fun hobby, right? And don't say you're under twenty-one. The law's eighteen here, and I'm pretty sure you're all adults, anyway."

Mom would absolutely freak, but somehow that fact emboldens

me. I bring the bottle to my lips and tip my head back. The bitter taste of the beer coats my tongue. "It's . . . stale, but refreshing?"

How do Vietnamese uncles from Little Saigon drink this?

The worker comes out of the stall and drops two full plates of food in front of us. The sweet-and-sour aroma wafts around the tables, making everyone drool.

I recognize the ingredients immediately. Mom always stocks the fridge with the same Vietnamese staples. Her taste buds since Việt Nam remain unchanged, save for her obsession with our local pizzeria. The dishes look just like how Mom would make them. Periwinkle escargot in tamarind sauce. Sea snails in coconut milk and lemongrass. The exact meals she'd cook every Thanksgiving because we don't like turkey.

Did she learn how to make them here? From who? Did she grow up eating with friends just like this, too? Drinking stale beer under the Sài Gòn skyline?

"Everyone!" Nga calls. "Raise your beer and let's make a toast! Repeat after me. Một, hai, ba, dzô!"

One, two, three, drink, what a silly phrase. We each raise our bottles and clink them against each other. "Một, hai, ba, dzô!"

Nga beams. "To a semester of fun!"

"Wooo-hoooo!" Cindy cheers, jumping from her seat to dive into the food, knocking her beer onto my pants in the process. The pink blouse she's been wearing since we were in California is miraculously fine.

"Shit, Cindy!" I grumble. The dampness doesn't bother me, but it's my favorite pair of jeans. Jeans that Mom stayed up past 5:00 a.m. to hem just because I asked her to. Cindy fusses, wiping down my clothes with spare napkins from the table.

"It's fine."

She raises an eyebrow. "Uh, whenever you say that, it means that it's actually not fine."

"I'm going for a short walk to air-dry this. You guys eat first." So much for eating ốc xào. Mom's is better anyway.

I walk toward the river, watching the lights from the city bounce off the water. My eyes survey the sight in front of me: families laughing, children running up and down the sidewalks, students egging one another on. I stay there for a moment, watching these strangers in a city I've only been in fewer than eight hours.

Another message from Mom.

Mom: How's Singapore? Did con eat yet?

Yes. I had bánh mì, I start to type before remembering my lie. Do they even have bánh mì in Singapore? Never mind that, Mom would be asking all kinds of questions. I do a quick Google search of popular Singapore street food before settling on a lie. *Wonton mee.* I even attach a Google image before hitting send.

Mom: Ok. Stay safe.

So ominous. Part of me wishes I could send her photos of Sài Gòn. Talk to her about what a whirlwind my first day has been. Send photos of the food and of my friends. Tell her I know what nhậu is. I untuck the photograph of Mom in front of the cathedral from my wallet, letting the streetlight cast a glow over her face. She's pointing at something—laughing at someone behind the camera, and my heart lurches at that wide, open-mouthed smile in the photograph. I want to know about her life here, all the little stories and moments that I never knew growing up.

She wouldn't get it. After all, she kept all of this away from me.

I keep walking, still watching everyone that passes by me. I wonder if any of them are my family, if Mom's sister had just passed me without knowing, and if I'll ever meet the people in the photograph wedged between the edges of my wallet.

My right foot kicks something hard.

A notebook.

I pick it up and flip through the pages. Whoever wrote this scribbled out most of it, the black ink practically bleeding through the paper. A line catches my attention.

This park sells the best Cá Viên Chiên! The stuffed fish balls are sweet, spicy, and explode with roe when you chew. It's best to enjoy the delicious snack while watching the sunset with someone! The owner is a working mom with the cutest daughter. Whenever you get the chance to come to this park, do support them!

The very caption from the photo *A Bánh Mì for Two* posted on Instagram. Today. Hours ago. My heart pounds wildly in my chest. They were here—are they still here? A million thoughts are racing through my head. Where are they? Out of all these strangers, whose face belongs to the person that wrote the blog that made me want to come to Sài Gòn? I have to tell Cindy.

My feet pivot, and for the umpteenth time today, my body collides into someone.

Chapter Seven

LAN

My body meets something soft, a mixture of jasmine blossoms and citrus overwhelming my nose. Pain flares up in my ankles and I hiss. Blinking, my eyes adjust to the girl in front of me. High cheekbones, inky-black hair reflecting the glow of streetlights, and dimples. Dimples that move with every expression. Like right now, when her eyebrows crease and her eyes brighten as she looks at me.

"Trời ơi! I'm so sorry!" she exclaims in Vietnamese, her American accent coming through.

Again—what's with foreigners speaking to me in Vietnamese, then immediately following up with English? Just pick a damn language to butcher.

"I'm so sorry," she says again. A Vietnamese girl. Wait, the Vietnamese American girl from earlier. No wonder her Vietnamese sounded better than that white couple's.

"Are you okay?" She offers a hand.

Rubbing my bruised backside, I drag myself up and open my

mouth to say something, when my eyes zero in on the notebook at her side.

Scrambling, I snatch it back, gripping the leather binder against my chest and feeling its familiar weight as my heart pounds. "Where did you get this?" I ask in English.

She blinks. "It was on the ground . . ." She reaches for the notebook again, but I shove it behind my back. "Is it yours? If not, I'm returning it to its owner."

I sigh exaggeratedly. Great. "Of course it's mine! It's my handwriting *and* my notebook."

She chews on her bottom lip, crossing her arms. "Recite something you wrote, then."

I narrow my eyes. "You're kidding."

"I'm not. Prove to me that it's yours."

Huffing, I tap my feet. "I could run right now. I have the notebook." I should definitely run.

"I used to run in high school," she points out. I resist the urge to roll my eyes. What does an American brat have on me? "And I could scream that you stole it."

I gape at her, throwing my arms up defensively. It's my notebook. *She's* the one that stole it. "Fine. I wrote about coming to this park earlier and eating cá viên chiên. Is that enough?"

"Shit." Her eyes bulge, flickering up and down my body as the realization appears on her face and a huge smile blooms. "*You* are the blogger of *A Bánh Mì for Two*. I've been a big follower of the blog and I just can't believe I'm actually seeing you in person. I've read every single post and even have my notifications turned on for when you post and how come you haven't written in months—"

"No," I cut her off. "I'm not."

There's no harm in a stranger finding out, but at the same time, I'm not ready. Maybe I shouldn't have panicked and lied, but knowing that one of my readers is right here and in front of me is overwhelming. I'm scared. What if she's disappointed in me? What if I can't give her an answer on the whys and oh-but-when-will-you-start-writing-agains of my hiatus? Especially if the girl in front of me is *Evermore13*, who is supposedly in Việt Nam right now. I don't want to disappoint her—to have her know that I'm just a regular girl who was prettier in her head and not a have-it-all-together blogger with an idealized life.

I've already lied. There's no turning back now.

She chews on her bottom lip. "But . . . the Instagram caption. What you just said. This specific park. Everything matches. It's you. It's fate," she whispers.

Fate? I sigh in disbelief. "It's not me, okay?" I exhale deeply, raising my pitch. "Leave me alone."

"Wait—"

I turn on my heel, ready to run back to the tiny house with the mango trees.

The girl tugs at my arm instead, and I flinch at the skin-to-skin contact, goose bumps lining my arm while her gaze meets mine, unwavering. "I came to Sài Gòn because of you—your blog. You helped me understand how Việt Nam actually is, and your words convinced me to see my homeland for the first time. I don't know why you haven't written in so long, but I hope you know that your words have impacted so many people. And I'm one of them."

"It's not me," I tell her, and yank my arm away. The notebook tucked in my arms suddenly feels heavy, and my legs burn as I will my body to leave the park. I keep running, running, and running until the park is completely out of sight and my body's swallowed by the wave of motorbikes. All the while, her words echo in my ears and anxiety rises in my throat.

When the mango tree finally emerges, I squint into the shadows to see Triết kicking his legs absentmindedly on our swing. "You look like you've seen a ghost."

I touch my left cheek, shuddering at how cold it is. "I found it." I wave the notebook at him. "I'm going to bed."

"It's barely night."

I check my phone. 21:00. "So what?" I snap, immediately regretting it.

Triết whistles. "Geez, sorry."

"I crashed into someone at the park." I rub my neck, feeling guilty for snapping at him. My entire body feels awfully sweaty, and to make everything worse, dirt is streaked all over my legs.

He softens his eyes. "Go wash up. There's blood on your elbow."

I check and wince, annoyance boiling back up at the state of my body. This scratch is definitely going to hurt tomorrow.

Triết looks like he wants to say something. The classic Triết look of chewing on his nails whenever he's anxious.

"What's wrong?" I could wait until he tells me on his own time. But I also don't have time.

"Oh, nothing. Just anxious about my exam tomorrow."

He's a worse liar than me. There's a reason why he was waiting. This swing is our spot, where we'd sit and wait for each other whenever something was wrong; I did the same two years ago, when Triết found me crying after I had found out about my mom's health. Oftentimes, we don't say much—we just listen to each other.

I scoot next to him, lifting my legs onto the swing and holding them to my chest. "Stop stalling before I delete your gaming account."

He whistles. "These threats from you are getting more serious every day. But I was just thinking about how I'll be graduating soon."

"I know. Congrats." I mean these words. Triết worked so hard the past four years, always studying or doing homework while also helping us at the stall. He showed up at our door four years ago with only a backpack of clothes and an armful of books, telling us he's enrolling in aerospace engineering.

With a well-off family, he could go anywhere he wanted but chose to stay with us.

Má, of course, took him in without question. Like Ba, she looks out for anyone and everyone.

I'll take care of your mom, Triết had promised me.

I sigh, hugging my legs closer. "It's an exciting thing—why are you scared?"

"I feel stuck. All my classmates are doing internships with Boeing and international airlines . . . but I couldn't nab anything. No one would take a kid who needs to work another job for most of the week."

Oh. The bánh mì stall. Of course it's the bánh mì stall. When Ba passed, everything shifted to me. I couldn't cry, couldn't grieve—at least not in front of Má. I'm her only child, her only daughter, the only other family she has. Without Ba, it's been me and her against the world. Who else could shoulder these responsibilities if not me?

"I can handle it. You don't have to help out so much. Go get an internship. You didn't sign up for this."

Triết was one more mouth to feed, and yet Má still took him in. I wonder if it's because he's a boy—because I can't ever replace Ba for her.

"Shut up. You didn't sign up for this, either." He flicks my forehead and brings his legs to his chest, too. We sit side by side on the swing, feeling its motion rocking us back and forth under the mango tree. "I don't regret helping you and Aunt. Or feel bad about it, either. You're the only family I have in Sài Gòn, and I sure don't want to go back to Bến Tre."

"Don't you miss your family?" My question lingers between us. Triết seldom talks to his family, and when he does, it's often a phone call from one of his sisters. I never pry; we all have things we'd rather not say. "I'm sure they think of you. How you're doing in Sài Gòn. If you're all right."

"They know I'm alive. I think that's enough."

I inhale sharply. "But . . . don't you want to go home sometime?

The Mekong River . . . the floating market . . . it sounds so, I don't know, peaceful? Away from all this noise."

If I tell him that sometimes I dream of leaving Sài Gòn, what would he say?

He shrugs. "But this noise is what makes Sài Gòn, Sài Gòn."

"You sound like a tourist blog."

"Good. Hope I'm inspiring you."

I haul myself up from the swing, a slight grin on my face. "Good night. Lock the doors when you go to sleep."

"Lan?" he calls back.

"Yeah?"

"Thanks for listening to me . . . and just so you know: There's nothing wrong with wanting to leave your home—or growing tired of it."

"I never said anything about leaving Sài Gòn."

"I know. I'm just letting you know, that you can."

Sprawling out on my mattress in my room, I think about what Triết just said. I know his family from Bến Trè are farmers, and he grew up surrounded by orchards and rabbits and cows. He talked about it sometimes, how he'd hop boat to boat on the floating market on the Mekong in the morning before going for a swim in the afternoon. How sunlight feels warmer south of Sài Gòn and how plentiful the gardens are. Yet, he still left. There are so many reasons people leave the place they've grown up in. What makes a person leave? My thoughts wander to the Vietnamese American girl whose face I keep seeing in my mind. Even now, as I lie in the dark, I can still hear her voice calling back to me from the park.

She's probably here because her family immigrated to the States. Or maybe she's one of those tourists that wants to "find themselves" in Sài Gòn. I roll my eyes at this thought.

The annoyance comes back. Why the hell do I keep thinking of her, anyway? She took Ba's notebook. To think I almost lost one of the only things left from him . . . to someone who never knew him at all.

How strange it is that something you hold so dear can mean nothing to another person.

"You're being ridiculous, Lan," I whisper to the dark.

Phan Ngọc Lan doesn't exist in the world of *A Bánh Mì for Two*. No one knows who Lan is except for the customers at Bánh Mì 98. Will I ever be more than that?

Chapter Eight

VIVI

I dream of Sài Gòn lights, cold beer, and the face behind the book-marked tabs on my laptop. I dream of her running away from me, and my hand reaching out—so close, but not enough—before she slips away.

My phone blares through the room and I groan into my pillow. I press the snooze button, slide the phone under the pillow, and roll onto my side. Just yesterday, I was in my own bedroom in California, and now I'm halfway across the world. Light streams through our thin window curtains, bringing noises from the street.

The door cracks open and Nga slips in, her hair damp. She massages her face with a wet towel and looks at me. "I know you're up, Vivi. I can hear that alarm from down the hall."

"But Ngaaaaa, five more minutes." Someone's chickens crow at 6:00 a.m. here, and the streets are loud through the night—how anyone expects my body to sleep well is beyond me.

I open an eyelid, and see her rolling her eyes at me. "It's already nine. You've been pressing snooze for the past hour. Those five minutes will turn into another hour and you're going to be upset when we're all eating bánh mì except you."

My stomach responds happily to the word *bánh mì* by letting out an embarrassingly loud grumble.

"It's the same bánh mì that you ate yesterday. I'm a regular there, and chị Lan makes the best breakfast bánh mì."

"Fine," I say. "Just because you've convinced me." Still, the word *bánh mì* reminds me of what had happened last night, and the hurt and *embarrassment* that followed when *she* ran off. Maybe it's my fault for daydreaming about my fateful meeting with the author of *A Bánh Mì for Two*. She looked . . . scared, though I guess I would be, too, if someone showed up, stole my notebook, and accused *me* of being the thief.

Oh, I was an ass.

"Now get up." Nga tugs at my arm and helps me out of bed. "Cindy's already complaining downstairs."

"Doesn't surprise me one bit."

I greet the busy streets of Sài Gòn from the sidewalks of our dormitory again. It's only half past nine in the morning, and still the sun shines relentless heat on my cheeks. A line of motorbikes and customers curves around the stall as people shout their orders. But even with so many customers, only three people are working—an elderly lady, a boy, and *her*. My heart skids to a halt when I catch sight of the girl from yesterday perched next to the bánh mì stall. She's wearing a hat today, shielding her face from the harsh sun. In the daylight, her skin shines golden and still glistens with sweat, but her braid looks the same, neat and dangling over her right shoulder.

That's why she was so scared. The author of my favorite blog is a street food seller. Her words on the blog suddenly have a new meaning. She wasn't just writing about the hardships and labor of street food that others face every day. She was writing about herself. No wonder she's so passionate about writing about street food, and no wonder she knows *so much* about it. Still, I wonder why she hasn't said anything about being a street food seller herself.

Her long-sleeved blouse sways with every movement, elongating her slender arms as I watch her go from slicing baguettes to pouring soy sauce. There's a rhythm to her movement, to the way her fingers pick through the ingredients like chords on an instrument. But her eyebrows scrunch with dismay, and despite her making each order effortlessly, there's an air of restlessness. The scorching sun highlights the beads of sweat on her face, and I have a weird urge to dab them away.

I continue stealing glances at her as we approach the front of the line. A stout lady grills meat behind her, and a smoky hint of charred pork wafts to my nose. I spy bánh mì crumbs on the girl, remembering how she left those crumbs on my shirt last night—like leaving a piece of who she is with me. I wonder how long she's been doing this. Selling street food, feeding people.

Nga, ahead of us, waves furiously at the girl. "Chị! Goooood morning! Can I have the usual? Oh! These are my friends!"

"Morning, Nga! One bánh mì chả lụa and one cup of cà phê sữa đá for you, then."

My eyes dart back and forth from Nga to the girl, watching them exchange Vietnamese fluidly with each other. The language rolls off their tongues like a song, and I realize I hadn't ever listened to Vietnamese without a sad tone. Mom likes talking in English and reserves Vietnamese for when she's upset or for words without translation.

"What about you?" the girl repeats in perfect English, her voice jolting me from my thoughts. Her expressions betray almost nothing, but there's a slight twitch in her temple. Does she remember me? Maybe I saw a different side of her yesterday, a glimpse into who she is apart from being a street food seller.

Flustered, I repeat the same order as Nga's.

Money already in hand, I pass her the bills, our fingers slightly brushing. I stare at her face as she takes the money, finding myself hoping for her to remember me. The scents of the grimy street and grilled meat surround us, clinging onto our clothes, and yet she exudes a woodsy smell, almost like a fresh summer rain. Suddenly I'm fully aware of the way my chest rises and falls.

"I'm sorry about last night." The words escape my mouth before I can stop myself. Cindy gapes at me, shock and confusion on her face, but the girl—she just stares at me, though I can see her mouth moving, teeth grinding against her cheek.

She breaks eye contact and digs into her pocket for my change. "Anything else?" She clears her throat, already looking past me to the next customer.

Still, I continue. "I was an ass. One hundred percent, and I should have trusted you and given you back the notebook right away."

She chews on her bottom lip, her eyes darting from the dirt between our feet to the notebook next to her on a plastic stool. The very same notebook from last night. With another inhale, I rehearse the words I've wanted to say for so long: "Thank you—for your blog, your stories. You've helped me a lot, more than you know. I'm staying right across the street and will probably come by often."

The girl finally meets my gaze, and my eyes snap to her lips as she silently sucks in a breath. "It's . . . okay. Thanks for reading, that's a really nice comment. And thanks for finding my notebook."

She hands me the plastic bags containing the food. I rush to help her with the drinks, our fingers skimming across each other; I almost drop the bags.

Without thinking, I blurt out. "What's your name?"

She blinks. "Lan."

Lan. Lan of Bánh Mì 98. Lan of *A Bánh Mì for Two.*

Chapter Nine

LAN

No one ever asks me for my name. The people of Sài Gòn stream through our stall like water, and no one stops long enough to bother. I recognized those dimples the moment *she* entered the line. My heart banged against my chest when I saw her move closer and closer. I prepared myself for more questions, even anger from the stranger, but it was something I hadn't expected: a girl insistent on the impact of my blog, even thanking me and saying sorry. She *did* ask me for my name, and I gave it to her.

Before I could ask for her name back, she had already hurried across the street and disappeared into the dormitory. I wonder if what she said is true, that she'll come by often. Maybe it would be nice to talk to someone my age that's not Triết.

I feel myself forgiving her for the notebook. It was the way she said it, how her eyes looked into mine with so much sincerity. How my writing affects her so much.

I peek at the notebook that's practically glued to my body now. The more I think about the contest, the *prize*, the more my head aches.

Má slices a mango next to me, skillfully taking apart all the juicy meat of the fruit from its seed. She hands me a piece and I pop it into my mouth. "Did you hear about Cô Châu's daughter? Trâm? The one who was in the same grade as you?"

Vietnamese mom gossip. Can always count on it. "No? What did she do this time? I remember her skipping school." Nothing gets Má—or any Vietnamese mom—more excited than gossip, especially if other people's problems are larger than ours. It's the only way Má and I communicate, anyway; it's easier to talk about someone else than about ourselves.

"Her kid ran away to Hà Nội last year! I didn't know." She shakes her head. "But she came back just yesterday. Looking all different, too! Her face is thinner, and her skin is more tanned. She's also enrolling at Hà Nội University."

"Wow. Good for her." No wonder she was the target of the community's gossip for the past year. Trâm was reserved in high school, eating lunch alone and never hanging out in the hallways after the last class. I should have said hi more. Maybe she was struggling. Maybe that's why she left.

"It's a miracle she turned out all right."

"All right? She's attending a prestigious university."

"You don't get it, con. In this life, family is all you have. How did she even make money to live there by herself? Who took care of her? Who housed her? Many bad things could have happened."

I can kiss my dream of traveling elsewhere goodbye, I guess. "At least she seems happier," I whisper.

We sit in silence again, the latest gossip not enough to sustain our strained relationship. Other people's problems don't matter at the end of the day if we're just playing pretend. There are so many things I should ask her—how she's doing, if she misses Ba like I do, and if she ever thinks about retiring the bánh mì stall—but I can't.

"You should go to school, Lan."

My gaze jerks up to Má. "What?"

Not this conversation again. Is this why she brought up Trâm?

Not looking at my face, she cuts open another mango, peeling the skin before answering me. "You were talking to the international students, weren't you? It's okay if you want to go to college. I can take care of the stall myself."

I look down at my sandals, gritting my teeth. My muscles feel tight and the sweat on my forehead suddenly becomes unbearable. I shake my head. "You're wrong, Má. College is unnecessary. And I'd be bored every day."

She makes a *tch* sound with her tongue. "But—"

"Má, I don't want to go."

Má sighs and closes her eyes. My stomach is in knots, tangled by shame and guilt and hurt. I hate lying to her. I hate that we always circle back to this conversation. I know Má would say that this is what Ba would have wanted me to do. But what Ba wanted doesn't matter anymore, especially now, because he's *not* here. I force myself to swallow the mango's sourness and the wave of grief threatening to overtake me.

"You can go rest, Má. Go have some lunch." I hand her a water bottle as an offering, an exchange of peace to let her know that I'm not mad—I never am. But I don't want to talk about university. I know it's a privilege to go, and *I should go.*

It's the right, linear life path. But what if I want to do something else? But that doesn't matter, because I need to focus on what's in front of me—the bánh mì stall. Family.

Má takes the bottle and reluctantly gets up. "Con, I worry about you sometimes. You push yourself very hard."

My chest throbs. "Má, you don't need to worry."

"But I have to. You're my daughter. My family."

I squeeze her hand. "I'll be okay. Remember to take your medicine after lunch."

She holds my gaze, squeezing my hand back. "Con, you don't have to worry so much. I'll be fine."

I swallow the lump in my throat, nodding as the warmth of her palm slips through mine. Right after Ba's accident, I often thought about scenarios where something really, really bad happened to Má and tried to figure out what I would do in that situation. Find the nearest clinic and the best nurses in case her pain worsens. Have the phone number of everyone she talks to. Try to text Triết every five minutes—I'd worry him sick with my antics.

With all my fussing, no wonder I wasn't the first person she told about her diagnosis.

I cool the beads of sweat on my neck with a damp cloth, my fingers clenching the material too tight. I scrub the towel on my face until my cheeks are raw. My eyes burn, and I slump my head onto my knees. Sài Gòn noises whirl by me, no one pausing to look. I feel small—just a girl on a plastic stool in the middle of one of the busiest cities in the world. Everyone has things to do, places to be. That American girl, she has somewhere to be, too. She's here for a short time before she goes home or maybe to a different city. She'll travel. See the world. Leave home. Find herself. Despite how much I envy her, my mind replays the small interaction between us. For once, someone cared enough to ask for my name. In that moment, I wasn't just a street food seller. I was Lan.

Chapter Ten

VIVI

Lan.

Orchid flower, according to Google. She fits her name, beautiful and elegant. I replay the moment her hand touched mine over and over. To put a face to all the bookmarked pages, to the Instagram I've looked at every day, and to the girl who brought me here—I can't even describe this feeling. But I remember how my breathing slowed as I watched her gracefully make bánh mì.

I roll into bed with a stupid smile on my face, my heart pounding at the thought of her . . . Of all her followers, she shared her name with *me*. Well, I did pry it out of her. But she still gave it to me, *so she trusts me*. Right? Either way, something changed—I felt it in the way her gaze softened at me, and how her mouth twitched when I started pouring my heart out to a stranger.

"I can't believe I'm saying this." Cindy snaps me from my thoughts. I had just finished explaining how I crashed into Lan last night and all the cosmic forces that led us to each other. Cindy plops next to me. "But maybe you were destined to meet.

"What's next?" she asks. "Your long-lost-but-not-really-lost family?"

"No, this was a once-in-a-lifetime kind of luck, so who knows if it'll happen again? Someone must be pulling miracles if I *do* find my mom's family."

"*Or* you could just ask your mom."

"That's a one-in-a-million chance of ever happening."

She rolls her eyes, laughing. "Well, at least now I'll still get to watch a beautiful friendship blossom between you and your favorite person in the world."

"Favorite person in the world?" I cringe. "You're so dramatic."

"You read her blog at least once a day, and I'm the only one who has to listen to you talk about it. Now I'm free—you can talk to her, and I'll be here watching and cheering." She giggles. "Maybe it's time for you to have some romance, too. Ask her on a date—"

"Are you kidding?" She cannot be serious. What if I scare Lan away? Plus, I don't even like her like that. "She's someone I respect . . . not a crush or whatever you think this is."

"Oookaaayyy. You can still respect someone and have a crush on them."

"That's not the point. Will you please help me photoshop myself in front of Singapore's Merlion instead of psychoanalyzing me?"

"Oh yeah. We still need to do that. Go stand over there." She positions me flat against the white dorm wall and gets into her "photographer" pose—something she lovingly named after seeing the way my dad takes photos: squatting as close to the ground as possible, butt back and the phone aligning to the perfect height. "Scoot closer to the window. We need the sun in your face or else it'll be too obvious."

I follow her direction. Chin up. Chin down. Turn to the side. Smile. Smile with teeth. No smiling too much. Pretend to point. "How many photos are you going to take?"

"Okay, the other wall next."

"*Seriously?*"

She shrugs. "You can't rush art."

We finally settle on two "good enough" photos out of the five hundred we took. This whole scheme is going to use up all my phone storage. Cindy carefully cuts out my silhouette and places it just at the right angle beside the Merlion, turning up the exposure and saturation for a warm tone. "There," she says, proud of herself. "You look like a tourist. Mission accomplished."

My mouth falls agape at the photo. She even photoshopped flyaway hair to my face so it looks like we're actually outside. "You can start a business out of this."

"You can help me with the taxes."

I roll my eyes. "Just because I've been helping my immigrant parents with their taxes since birth doesn't mean I'm obligated to do yours."

"You're forgetting that I've also been doing my immigrant parents' taxes since I was in the womb. Surprised the IRS hasn't come after us yet. Speaking of immigrant parents, your mom's calling."

"Shit. Shit. *Shit*. It's a FaceTime! What the fuck do I do?"

"Quick! Get in bed." She pushes me toward the bed before helping me position the sheets over half of my face. "And make sure only your face is in the frame. Facebook mom–style."

The FaceTime connects. "Vivi!" Mom's voice comes through, and instantly I see her face with the way she looks whenever she's concerned and about to flip mountains. Both eyebrows raised and lips thinned. "You took long."

"Yeah, sorry, Mom, was asleep." I fake a yawn. "Jet lag, you know?"

"Okay, con . . . What did you do on your first day? Tell Mommy." Since Mom immigrated at a young age, she often speaks to me in a mix of Vietnamese and English. She often trades a word in one language for a word in the other when she can't remember the right vocabulary. She refers to herself as Mommy. I could call her Mẹ, but the Vietnamese word basically means the same thing, anyway. Vietnamese is strange like that—there's no universal pronoun for I. Even I call myself *con*, which directly translates to "child." I was taught to always use *con* when talking to someone older than me. "Is that a pimple? Tch, Mommy biết Asia can be so stressful on you. Your face is red like trái tomato."

"What? No, it's a mosquito bite—"

"Mosquitoes! What kind of place have con muỗi? Where are you staying?"

"A good and expensive place!" Mom strangely only approves of anything that has a hefty price tag to it. The more expensive it was, the more she'd trust it. "And my first day was good. I had ốc xào—"

Cindy taps her foot and furiously shakes her head at me. "Vivi! What did we talk about? No mentioning anything related to, you know, your *homeland*?" she whisper-yells.

Mom's brows deepen. "Ốc xào?"

I let out a loud laugh. Too loud. "Why did I say that! Um, I had some lo mein!" Is lo mein popular in Singapore? "I said ốc xào because I missed your ốc xào so much, Mommy."

She cracks a smile. "Come home soon, con. Mommy can make it for you." Feeling unexpectedly brave after seeing her happy, I brace myself. "Mom . . ."

"What?" The crinkled brows are back.

"How would you feel if I . . . say, take a flight from Singapore to Việt Nam? I mean, it's so close, and this can be a chance for me to . . ."

Cindy stares at me like I just lost my mind. I also can't believe I just asked Mom this.

"No." The smile isn't there anymore.

"But Cindy can come with me!"

"No. Absolutely not. Who is going to take care of you? You can get killed."

Twenty-four hours here and I'm still very much alive.

"Why do you hate Việt Nam so much?" I whisper, and the line goes silent as I see Mom grind her teeth, veins surfacing on her face.

"Con," she sighs. I prepare for Mom to shut me down, to tell me the usual whys: that I'm too young, too little to understand. But that doesn't come. "Việt Nam is very unsafe. Bad people live there. And . . . you can get hurt." I can hear the anxiety behind her words.

"Mommy have to go make dinner," she continues. "Mommy thương con rất nhiều. Con stay safe—okay? And don't talk to strangers!"

Oops. "Okay, bye, Mommy."

Cindy saunters over to my bed and lets out a big sigh. "That went well."

"So, so well." I nod. "I'm so glad my parents don't know how to track my location. Can you imagine how my mom would react if she ever found out?"

"I don't need to imagine." She shudders. "I *know.*"

"I can't believe you lied to your parents for me."

"What can I say? I'm your best friend, and unfortunately for my parents, they got a rebellious spirit instead of a good Catholic girl."

I cackle. "I can't believe they all forced us to go to Sunday school for so long."

"Don't remind me." She plays with the cross necklace that her parents insist on her wearing on this trip to protect her. Our parents are too alike. "Remember how they were whenever we talked about gay rights?"

"Yes! I was so passionate, they should have known I was gay then."

I prop my head up on my arm. "What are the chances I can become friends with Lan if I just stare at her from the window every day?"

"That is so creepy, and you know it. Talk to her—"

"It's not that I don't want to talk to her . . . It's that I feel so bad about lying to my mom! Did you hear what she said? Don't talk to strangers! She's told me that twice since we got here. I'm convinced she taped a camera to me."

"Vivi." She takes my hand before looking into my eyes. "If you felt bad about lying, this trip wouldn't have happened in the first place.

"Fuck it," she continues. "Your mom hasn't suspected anything. You just need to stop saying the first thing that comes to your mind and never mention Việt Nam in front of her . . . We're set!"

I guess she has a point.

"And technically Lan isn't a stranger. You've known her before this."

"Known *of* her. But fine, I'll talk to her. What do I have to lose?"

She hums. "Yeah. Not like you'll fall in love with her and beg to stay in Sài Gòn after our study abroad."

Chapter Eleven

LAN

The sun shines through our small backyard as morning dew gathers on Ba's orchids and herbs. Ba chose the name Lan because of the orchids all over our house. I water them and pluck the herbs for the day as Má and Triết lug our cart toward the front of the house. Closing the door behind me, I give the family photo a kiss and pack our condensed milk and patê. I race down our alleyway and toward the smell of buttery bread, toward the Lê Bakery, which has probably fed half of Sài Gòn by now, operating for over fifty years. Every morning, I grab fresh loaves for the bánh mì stall. But today, instead of taking my usual route, I turn down a different alley-way tucked between tall buildings made of concrete slabs, plants growing over the weather-stained walls between units.

Aha.

A wooden door to the building was left slightly ajar, so I slip through and find myself staring at a familiar sight: a shabby, winding staircase that smells like mildew, the clouds looming at the very top. A secret passage to my very own rooftop overlooking all of Sài Gòn.

As I hike up these stairs, I wonder how old this building is, and what caused these stains. Finally, I duck through the flimsy door at the top and watch the city wake.

The plumeria tree emerging from one of the windowpanes greets me with its morning dew, and I pluck a flower, tucking it into my pocket before settling beneath the tree. It's all right. Just a moment. Everyone seems so small from up here. So small that I can't wrap my head around the fact that I, too, am a part of that small world in this big city.

"I had a feeling you'd be here."

A shadow towers over me. I look up and see Chú Hai, the oldest son of the Lê family, his eyebrows scrunching together.

"How'd you know about this spot?"

He shrugs. "Been alive in Sài Gòn for too long."

Chú Hai sets down his plastic bag and takes a seat next to me. He digs into the plastic bag and hands me a bánh patê sô. They are Ba's favorite, and mine.

I take a bite. The pork pastry immediately melts into my taste buds with its rich and salty flavor, while the flakes smear across my lips. "Yup. I'll need baguettes from you for the next fifty or sixty years."

"You know, we used to do this all the time, come to this spot. Me and your dad. This was our secret place."

"I didn't know that." It makes sense, Ba was the one who showed me this rooftop.

With the mention of Ba comes that familiar aching feeling settling over me, and the buttery pastry suddenly feels dry on my tongue. Aside from Má and me, the Lê family probably misses Ba the most. Ba went to school with everyone, and Chú Hai was his best friend. Even though Chú Hai's name is Bình, Ba and he were so close that I just call him Chú Hai—honorific for the eldest son and, in my case, uncle. When Ba passed, the neighbors showered me and Má with food, fruits, and even money they could hardly afford to give away. We weren't the only ones grieving—so was the entire community.

"We also used to sneak into the schoolyard at night with a vintage telescope so old that it was hardly usable. I had no idea where your dad got it from. Everyone knows that he loved literature, but the stars fascinated him the most. He would ramble on and on about the world beyond us. It seemed so unimportant to me at the time because it wasn't like we could do it. Go to space, I mean. Our dreams were on the ground."

My head suddenly feels heavy, so I rub my temple, my back finding the comfort of the concrete as I continue to look at the skyline with Chú Hai. "I remember Ba would look at everything in the sky and point it out to me."

Chú Hai chuckles, taking a bite of his own bánh patê sô. He wipes his hand and lies down next to me. "I can still remember the day that you were born. Your dad ran into the bakery teary with the biggest smile on his face. He said that the star that he had been searching for is here. That you were the brightest star of his life."

Tears prick at the corners of my eyes. Unable to say anything, I just let them fall. I concentrate on the sun, the chirping birds, and the loud city. No matter how many stories everyone tells me about Ba, he's still gone. I only have Má, and with just the two of us, she needs me more than anyone ever knows.

"Whenever you're ready, Lan," he breaks the silence. "Come grab the books your dad wanted you to have. Only if you're ready."

Ba had a lot of books, so many that he started storing some at Chú Hai's place as an extra library. I was supposed to pick up these books years ago, but I've found every excuse not to. Too busy tending the stall, not enough time, me being forgetful—I know Chú Hai knows they're all lies. Shame glooms over me, what a simple task that I can't bring myself to do. I do want the books; to hold them, feel their weight, and read the notes Ba left behind.

But I'm not ready, and I'm not sure if I'll ever be.

Dusting off the dirt on my pants, I sigh and stand up as I swallow the last bite of the bánh patê sô and all the grief in my throat. "Thanks. I'll remember this time."

Waving goodbye to Chú Hai, I finally stop by the bakery before racing to the bánh mì stall with the baguettes. To make matters worse, Triết hands me the wrong smoothie order. "This isn't mango."

He rolls his eyes and throws a towel at me to clean the plastic tables. "Mango, pineapple, whatever. Same thing. They're both yellow and fruit."

"Are you kidding me? Top of your class with this mentality?"

"Come on. You know I panic easily. I just pointed to the first yellow thing I saw. Forgive me?"

It's true. That's why I'm the one that takes orders. "How are things . . . with college?"

He quirks an eyebrow. "First time you're asking me about college."

"Sorry. I should try to ask you about these things more."

"I'm kidding. Thanks for asking anyway." He shrugs and helps me untie the plastic notch. "Still getting rejected from internships and the exams are going to kick my butt. It can only go up from here, right?"

"Guess so. Ready?" I ask, already spying the incoming tide of customers. Soon, the line will wrap around the neighborhood.

"More than ready. Let's give them the best bánh mì in Sài Gòn."

Bánh Mì 98 was always our family's. Ba's parents ran it. His parents' parents ran it. A small street food stand in the heart of Sài Gòn. When Ba took over, people raved all across the city and Bánh Mì 98 became synonymous with him and his food.

Ba loved trying new things. We'd wake up every weekend to the smell of fresh baguettes and something savory, and he'd tell us what the experiment was for the day. Bánh xèo in a bánh mì. Bánh mì with phở noodles. Sometimes he'd even make American food with a Vietnamese twist, like cá viên chiên on pizza with bánh mì as the crust. Má liked his inventions, but I *loved* them. He showed me that things were possible, limitless, and his love for food kept us going. Now we wake up to a lonely house with no smell of baguettes.

Triết nudges me. "Isn't that the girl that asked for your name?"

I jerk my gaze to the American girl near the back of the line. Our eyes meet for a second before I turn away. "How did you know that?"

"Good hearing. Got it from working and studying right here. So, what's going on?"

"*Nothing* is going on."

He picks at a piece of thịt nướng before eating it. "Considering you don't have any friends, that's a big deal."

My face burns. "I do have friends. You."

He cringes. "My point exactly. She's American, huh? You could use some international friends. Ask for her opinion on . . . food?"

"Not a chance."

But he does have a point. She obviously has been to more places than I ever have if she's here. Maybe I can ask about other cities, food, and cultures for the blog contest. "*Ugh*, the blog contest," I mutter to myself.

"What contest?" he asks.

Right, I haven't told anyone. "Someone sent me a submission call the other day. The *Southeast Asia Travel Magazine* is asking for pieces about the Most Beautiful City in the World. Winner takes home *a lot* of money."

"Sweet." He whistles. "Do it. You'll win."

I glare at him. "How are you so confident?"

"Are you kidding? You're a good writer and you have passion. I've never seen someone light up so much talking about food before."

But what can passion buy us? Even if I enter the competition, I probably won't win. "I'll think about it." Part of me had already made peace with not entering, but then I'd think about how happy Má would be if I won. She could rest, not feel bad about buying medicine for herself, and she'd be *proud* of me. If I win, then maybe writing can be a serious business for me—for us—and maybe then we wouldn't need the bánh mì stall anymore. Má wouldn't be out in the heat, wouldn't be massaging the aches in her joints.

Still, who would we be as a family without Bánh Mì 98? This stall was Ba's, and everyone else's that came before me. I can't just give up on it.

"You might want to stop thinking so hard and scrunching your eyebrows because the American girl looks like she really wants to talk to you," he whispers, just in time for me to see that she's literally in front of us.

Here we go again. I make sure my face is as neutral as possible with only a slight smile at the corner of my lips.

Bracing myself, I say the line I'll probably repeat the most in this life: "What can I get for you?"

"Hey," she says, practically vibrating. "Can I have two bánh mì thịt nướng?"

"Got that, Triết?" I clear my throat, not sure what to say. Should I make small talk? Tell her I forgive her and the whole notebook thing was so stupid anyway? No, I shouldn't bring it up again. I'd look like I've been spending too much time thinking about it—thinking about her. But my heart won't stop pounding, and though I want to look *anywhere else*, my eyes won't stop flickering to her face. It's like I'm almost forgetting we're in the middle of a busy city, and it's not just us but also her and her friend next to her—who's too busy taking photos of the bánh mì lined perfectly in the bánh mì cart.

He nods and gives me a thumbs-up. It usually only takes minutes to prepare an order, but time moves too slow today.

The girl is looking everywhere but my eyes—my entire face, actually—and keeps fidgeting with her hands. But I'm doing the same, just picking at my own cuticles. Maybe I should just wait this out, what's the point of making friends, anyway. I'm here to do one thing: to sell food, and she's a customer. Just another person in Sài Gòn who will soon leave.

"Hot today," she says. "Rất nóng."

My usual annoyance about tourists flip-flopping between English and Vietnamese fades the moment my eyes meet hers again. Those big round eyes. "Dạ. Coi chừng nha, nóng lắm đó."

She brightens immediately at my Vietnamese, her voice squeaky. "Thank you! I'll make sure to be careful. The sun is so much hotter here."

"You switched back to English," I say, finding her clumsiness somehow endearing. "But I'm surprised you understood me."

Her smile widens. "I'm not that confident in my speaking abilities. But I can listen just fine—"

A customer cuts in front of her before promptly shoving cash in my face, tenfold of the listed price on the bánh mì cart. I mentally roll my eyes, another tourist. "Hey, can I get a bánh mì with no meat? Oh, actually, do you have Impossible meat? And no soy sauce. What's the pickle thing?" He starts firing rapid English at me, and what the fuck does "impossible meat" even mean?

"Dude. I'm waiting on my order," the girl speaks back. A smile tugs at my lips. I guess she's not all that squeaky.

"Perfect! You already ordered. She can take mine right away," he says before turning back to me. "Is this enough money? I don't know how currency conversion works. Too much math."

I roll my eyes, *really* roll them. Calculators and the internet exist for a reason.

"There's a line," she retorts before I can say anything. Even Triết stops bagging her order to watch. We always had to deal with ridiculous customers ourselves, and though this happens on the daily, no one ever bothered to step in. And why would they? This is Sài Gòn, and we're just a tiny part of it. "You can't just cut like that. It's rude."

"Listen here, young lady. I have things to do, so I'd really appreciate it if the little girl can take my order and then I can get out of your way. Then we'd all be happy!"

My face twitches and I lightly slap my wrist before nasty words slip out of me. I should just let it go—there's no use in fighting something so stupid. I'll take his order and get this over with.

But the girl won't relent. "You can wait."

Even her friend joins in. "Get back there, asshole."

I smirk to myself. Americans sure have guts, even if they're seemingly small and not at all frightening. "Yeah, sorry. It's pretty long, but I'm sure you can wait."

"You speak perfect English!" He looks *shocked*.

"Why does that matter?" the girl and I say at the same time.

"Okay, you're a total dick. I get it. That's why you cut and shoved me out of the way. You think you run the world because you're tall, speak English, and aren't Asian," she continues.

"You know what? Fuck this bánh mì stall. And fuck you. I will not be coming back here ever again with this kind of customer service," he shouts before walking away.

"Pretty sure his temper tantrum is futile because . . . it seems the locals here really don't care," her friend says. A foreign face. Brown hair and brown eyes. "See? No one's even looking."

She's right. It's just another day for people in Sài Gòn. "Thank you." I hand the girl her order, and our hands brush once again. There's a flutter—a spark—so faint I almost miss it, until I look up into her eyes. Bright and wide, her face eclipsing the sun.

"What's your name?"

"Vivi." She smiles, clutching the food—*my food*—so close to her chest. "This is the best bánh mì in Sài Gòn."

Chapter Twelve

VIVI

"So, after spending so much money buying bánh mì . . . you want to waste more on books?"

"My two true loves in this life. *Please*, you promised me we'd go." I sit up on the bed, admiring Cindy in the flouncy white dress she picked up from the boutique next door. "Anyway, back to the topic at hand: Lan asked me for my name! Can you believe that?"

"*Yes*, Vivi! You've been subjecting me to the same conversation for the past forty-eight hours. And I've been coming along with you every time you 'crave bánh mì.' She asked you for your name and you still haven't tried asking her anything else. The ball's in *your* court now."

"It's hard!" I whine. "There's always such a long line and I feel bad about holding people up. I have anxiety!"

I wish I had a dollar for every time Cindy rolls her eyes at me. "I can't believe I'm going to spend the rest of this trip following you around to the bánh mì stall across the street. I want my own romance!" she says, clutching her chest.

"Someone's watching too many study abroad rom-coms." I can't blame her, though, the shows and movies did get the sense of feeling out of place right—but I'm not a tacky American. Am I?

"Oh shit!" A text from Mom comes through. "My mom's asking for more photos. What should I do?"

"Hmm." She purses her lips. "Fine. Let's take some photos near the bookstores you wanted to go to. Natural light and no need for me to photoshop. Easy."

"Won't she . . . notice something's off?"

She shrugs. "Not if we go to a modern bookstore and only pose with English books?"

"Good point."

Đường sách Nguyễn Văn Bình is a dream. A street lined with bookstores. The smell of paper, both fresh and old, tickles my nose as we walk into a store filled with twinkling lights. From Vietnamese literature to graphic novels, stationery, English books, and *more*. I float through the rows and catalog where different genres are. Colorful paper lanterns hang from the ceiling, softly glowing against the incandescent light. They look like constellations, and as they twinkle at me, I'm reminded of home—of my bedroom in Little Saigon full of bookshelves Mom and Dad built for me, and of the paper lanterns Mom likes to hang around our home. Then it hits me: This will be the first Trung Thu, first Mid-Autumn festival, that I won't be home for.

Cindy skips toward me, her arms full of journals. "I have to say that the Google reviews and your glowing recommendation were right. I could live here."

I smile. "I told you!"

She raises her arms, sighing. "Yes, I accept defeat."

"Good." I laugh. "Now that we've taken more than enough pictures for my mom, I'm going to look at more English books at another store!"

"Be careful!"

"You sound too much like like my mom!"

I step out and continue down Nguyễn Văn Bình Street, glancing at the city-goers alongside me. There are at least twenty bookstores on this street, each one unique and vibrant. I choose a bookstore next to a hoa phượng tree and peek inside. The sun glows against the pastel-colored walls. A couple canvases are displayed outside, showcasing paintings bursting with colors.

I marvel at the space, a tiny and cozy lounge with free assortments of mooncakes and tea. I grab a thriller novel before settling into a wooden chair. There are small private spaces separated by partitions on both sides, almost like library cubicles. The partitions can't drown out the furious typing from the person to my right, though. I try to concentrate, tracing the words with my index finger, but the smacking sound of fingers against the keyboard continues, relentless.

I inhale deeply, opening my mouth, then closing it immediately at the sight of the familiar braid. *Her.*

A dark green blazer hugs her body, and a faint blush paints her cheeks. No food-stained clothes. No worn sandals. This is a different Lan.

Her eyebrows scrunch, her eyes engrossed in the document she has open. Holding my breath, I arch farther back, straining my body to peek at the computer screen. My heart stops.

Southeast Asia Travel Magazine Open Call Submission.

She left the private message on read, so I had assumed she didn't want to write. But if she's typing . . . she has to be entering the competition. My heart pounds faster. She's *writing* again. But for every sentence she puts down, she hits backspace right away. I crane my body farther, inch the divider between the cubicles back to reveal more of Lan. Not realizing the distance thinning between us, I accidentally swipe my elbow against hers, the friction sending goose bumps up my skin. She yelps and jolts up immediately, sending my chair tipping to the ground and me crashing along with it. I brace for the fall and a potential concussion.

But it doesn't come. Instead, Lan grips my right arm as my head hovers slightly above the floor.

Eyes still closed, I clutch her forearm, flustered. "Thank you."

Lan's staring at me, and I can see red flaring across her face before she snatches her arm away, widening the distance between us again. "Um. Hi," she says. "You can have the space—I was just leaving."

Great. After all the progress I made after the notebook incident, I still look like a stalker she needs to run away from. "No, no, it's okay." Frantic, I say, "*I* was just leaving, anyway. You can finish up writing the open call submission—"

Shit.

Why did I say that?

Her eyes dart from her computer screen to me. "What about the open call submission . . ."

I stand up straighter. Maybe it is fate. Maybe something in the sky is conspiring for us to meet again and again—or maybe it's only accidental—but somehow I ran into her while she was working on the submission post. Maybe I can help?

"I sent you that private message, about the call, and saw you working on it earlier."

"*You* sent me the call?" she said, her eyes bulging. "*You're* Evermore13? Why didn't I put two and two together?"

"I want to help you write the story."

"How?"

"I can . . ." I hesitate. What *can* I offer Lan? What do I know that she doesn't? She's the one living in this city, breathing in what Sài Gòn has to offer. But maybe, just maybe . . . I can help, too. "Help you write something new about Sài Gòn from a different perspective. I'm a big reader, fluent in English, got a five on my AP Language test—not that any of this is *impressive*—but all I'm saying is, I really want to help. *Please* let me help."

She inhales deeply, eyes looking everywhere but at me. "Why do you want to help me? Are we going to split the prize—"

"No." I shake my head. "You can keep the entire prize. But what I told you the other day was true. I don't know why you haven't written in so long, and I won't ask, but I know that you run one of the best blogs out there."

She doesn't say anything, still staring at the words on her computer screen, lost in thought.

"You move people with your words, Lan. There's no way anyone would win but you. The magazine would be *lucky* to have your post featured."

I didn't expect Lan to doubt herself, too. All this time, I imagined her as someone who always gets what she wants, someone who's never afraid to speak her mind and carry herself with confidence—much like the conviction she exudes throughout her blog. But maybe she's like me. A girl with just as many insecurities as anyone else.

She relaxes her temple, the corners of her lips curving upward. "Okay. We can try, but there's no guarantee I can even write a blog post by the deadline."

My breath quickens. She agrees. She wants my help. I'm helping her, I'm helping *A Bánh Mì for Two*. "We'll take it slow—work at your pace."

She sighs. "Well, I haven't written anything at all."

"That's fine. You just need some inspiration, something to really kick your brain into gear."

"So, where do we start?"

I point to the book on her desk next to a stack of research materials about Sài Gòn, *First Timer in Việt Nam Travel Guide*. "Let's see what other people have said about Sài Gòn first."

"I did that already." She shrugs. "Nothing helps. Foreigners think of Sài Gòn as a—"

"*Playground*." I smile at her shocked face. "I know. I'm one of your biggest fans, remember? But it's still helpful to read all the good *and* the bad."

"Fine," she mumbles, and crouches down next to me, making my heart leap—her shoulder inches from mine. I can't help but notice her body language, the way she glides her pen across paper, how she whispers aloud as she reads.

"How come you've never asked me why I speak English so well?" Lan breaks the silence.

"I know you're fluent." I lift an eyebrow. "From your blog."

"Oh. Right."

"Plus, it's a weird thing to ask. People act like English is the superior language. Like being able to speak it means you're better than everyone or something." I roll my eyes.

Lan looks at me oddly before her lips curve and she *laughs*. "It's the first thing most foreigners ask! After making English the universal language, they act so surprised seeing fluent people in foreign countries. As if we weren't forced to take English in school to graduate."

"You said my Vietnamese was good—is that true?"

"I was impressed, but I didn't say good." Seeing my crestfallen face, she adds, "Kidding. Your Vietnamese sounds better than most Americans.'"

I grin, thankful that Cindy and I pooled our money together and found ourselves a Vietnamese tutor before studying abroad. I passed the class with flying colors. Cindy? Not so much.

"Even though I was raised by Vietnamese parents, they never took me to language schools on weekends," I admit. "So I took an eight-week class before coming, and was able to learn faster than most beginners since everyone speaks Vietnamese in Little Saigon."

We're closer than ever now, our elbows touching and our faces several inches apart. "Tell me about Little Saigon." Her breath dances on my lips. My breathing shortens, and my heartbeat pounds in my ears as I watch her eyes move across my features, as if she's studying every part of me.

"It's this . . . really small but also really big community in California. A lot of Vietnamese people live there, but I don't think they have always been there. From what I learned, most Vietnamese came in 1970s and 1980s after, um, the war."

She nods slowly. "I've heard about it. Why does everyone speak Vietnamese? Don't you have to learn English?"

"You don't! There's a Vietnamese version of everything. Most of the staff in the local coffee shops, tax offices, and even schools often speak and understand Vietnamese. We even have Vietnamese driving schools, where they teach you how to drive a car and get your license . . . in Vietnamese!"

"Wow. I can't even imagine that—a giant Vietnamese city outside of Việt Nam. It sounds so *cool*."

I tear my gaze away from hers, cheeks hot. "No one's said that before or described Little Saigon with awe."

"Why not?" The crinkled eyebrows resurface, and her eyes lock into mine, genuinely curious. "I want to see more Sài Gòns in the world. The Sài Gòn beyond this Sài Gòn. Vietnamese restaurants in Laos. In France. In America."

My heart thumps. "One day, I'll show you my Little Saigon. I promise."

"Better keep your promise," she says, her eyes twinkling.

Chapter Thirteen

LAN

A fluttering feeling makes its way from my chest to my arms, my legs, and my unsteady fingers. I peek at Vivi through the front strands of my hair, noticing the way her chest rises and falls.

"Do you want to go somewhere else?" I blurt out. The stuffiness of the space isn't helping, and I find myself curious about the girl next to me instead of doing whatever research we're supposed to do.

She lifts an eyebrow. "Sure! Where?"

"There's a café nearby that's really cute and has the best egg coffee—why don't we go there? And maybe try brainstorming?"

"Lan," she says, and my chest flutters again. I like the way she smiles when she says my name. "I've dreamed of this moment. One thousand percent yes. Never thought I'd be going on a food adventure with my favorite food blogger."

I swallow. Because I've kept the blog so private, no one's ever told me these things to my face before. All the comments were on a screen, with a gap just wide enough for me to convince myself that the kind words held no true meaning. But with Vivi, there's sincerity in her eyes, and *adoration*. My heart squeezes. "That's a big compliment."

"I'm not trying to kiss ass—wait, do you know what that means—"

"Yes." I roll my eyes. "I know basic American phrases."

She laughs, her dimples making an appearance again. "Just making sure."

Café 1975 always looks like a scene from Studio Ghibli. A quaint coffee shop tucked between modern buildings with its rusty blue and patterned-grille doors. I often found myself here after school. The afternoon sun invites itself into the space, rays the color of brewed tea. Vinyls line the wall and the record table plays a remastered ABBA album.

"Whoa, I feel like I'm inside a Hayao Miyazaki film," Vivi says, her mouth hanging.

"Right? It's so—"

"Whimsical," she finishes before bolting to the cash register.

Café 1975 was my little secret—well, not so much a secret since it is on a busy street, but it's not something I ever posted about. Or told anyone about—even Triết. When I was still blogging, it was hard to find somewhere just for myself. Somewhere I didn't feel pressure to write a blog post about. The last time I was here was Ba's first day of remembrance—ngày giỗ, or his death anniversary, when it clicked that he was never going to come back, and that the mango tree and orchids and our small garden would never feel his presence again. I sat in the farthest corner and pretended to look at their menu, my only friends the vinyls, ABBA, and old books. I couldn't even cry.

Now I'm back, and I brought someone. But Vivi's presence doesn't bother me. She makes the place look brighter.

"Why the blazer and trousers?"

I blink. "Oh. Right. You've only seen me in my usual black shirt and jeans at the bánh mì stall. It's kind of stupid, but I'm trying to convince myself that wearing nice clothes will make me more productive. It's not working too well, though."

She shrugs, grinning. "I think you look nice."

We're seated by the hoa phượng tree just outside the café. Its red petals dance around us before falling onto the concrete. Vivi settles in a wicker chair and plays with the fallen petals. She tucks a flower behind her ear, making my eyes wander to her cheeks—flushed, like mine.

Clearing my throat, I grab another petal from the ground and press it between the pages of my book. "Here. Vietnamese people like to press these flowers and turn them into bookmarks."

She immediately plucks more petals from the ground before promptly squashing them inside her book. "That's so cool! Now I can keep these with me forever."

"All my books have hoa phượng in them." Ba would always grab a handful for me off the schoolyard when he'd pick me up. *Look, this flower has a skirt*, he would joke. I swallow the rising grief in my throat and, instead, try to inhale the egg coffee's smell.

She twirls the blossoms between her fingers. "What kind of books do you like?"

Ba's books, and my own, haven't been touched since his passing. I almost wanted to throw them out. But instead of telling Vivi that I don't read anymore, I decide to just pretend; it's easier than explaining all the whys.

"I love stories that I can lose myself in. To escape reality and be whisked away to another world. Stories that make me root for the characters and make me feel like I'm part of something bigger than myself."

She sighs dreamily, her round eyes sparkling at the sky. "Isn't that the best part about books? The limitless things you can imagine in your head. All the places you could be."

I focus on stirring my coffee, allowing the words I've long repressed to come out.

"I loved books because of my dad. I never even planned for *A Bánh Mì for Two* to happen, or to have this many followers. I needed to write a story for a class about anything, so I chose to do it about street food and asked my dad to help me. He agreed and it became our little project. For the first two years, we wrote silly things together, not caring about anyone's opinion on the blog. Then he passed, and I kept writing, but this past year . . . I've been struggling with writer's block."

I'm not sure why I'm recounting my most vulnerable memories to someone I've just met, but Vivi should have all the details she can get about the blog to help. And it feels easy, less lonely, to talk to her. Maybe it's because I don't know her, and she doesn't know me.

"I'm sorry about your dad."

The same words everyone keeps telling me. What are they sorry for? What's *Vivi* sorry for? She wasn't there. We're just two lives colliding, dominoes cascading into place. And now I'm participating in a project with a stranger, with fleeting hope in my chest that somehow we'll win. That I *can* overcome this writer's block, and that Má will say, *I'm proud.*

She continues before I can speak. "I can feel the heart behind your words. How *A Bánh Mì for Two* is more than just a blog, and how much it means to you."

Unlike other people, she doesn't linger in her pity for me. She just . . . moves on. She doesn't pry into how I'm feeling or how I'm doing. It feels *nice.* Like I don't need to cut myself open and show her all the emotions stored within me.

Instead of wanting to shrink under the weight of her gaze, I feel myself basking in it, almost wanting *more.*

"I read the blog posts 'Recipes for a Big Dinner' and 'Places to Eat with a Huge Family' and daydreamed about being in Sài Gòn, sharing meals with my mom and dad. I'm sure, wherever your dad is, that he would be proud to know you're entering this contest."

Would he?

"Thank you." My chest feels light, and I smile back at her. It's impressive she can recite my blog posts back to me.

"Why'd you choose the name *A Bánh Mì for Two*? I don't think you've ever explained it on the site."

"Because food is always meant to be shared," I answer immediately. "At least in a lot of Asian cultures, everyone gets their own bowl while we pick off different plates in front of us. The same goes for street food. The name also comes from my dad. We'd order a bánh mì for two, splitting each half."

"My mom gets really excited when we go grocery shopping and restock our fridge. I think seeing the fridge full makes her happy, like we'll be full for another day. Maybe that's why I love your blog so much, because we both look at food . . . *beyond* food."

"I have to admit I never really thought that much about food and my blog. But this makes me really happy. You . . . get me."

Her eyes hold mine, unwavering. "I hope I do."

The coffee lingers on my tongue, and I realize how long it's been since I treated myself to a cup of egg coffee. How long it's been since I've sat down with someone my own age—besides Triết. "Thanks for picking up my notebook. If I hadn't run into you, I don't think I'd ever find the drive to enter this submission contest."

"Well, you *did* run away from me—but we're here. And I'm glad you're giving this whole thing a chance, giving *me* a chance to help you."

My chest warms, and part of me wonders what would happen had I never dropped that notebook; if Vivi's path never crossed mine, where would we be now?

"Is there anything you're hoping to see before you leave?"

She nods her head and takes out several photographs from her wallet before handing them to me. I hold them gingerly, noticing the creases on the flimsy paper. One is a photo of three women wearing beautiful áo dài standing in front of a tall, familiar building. They're hugging each other, smiling at the camera.

They all have the same eyebrows and nose as Vivi. The same smile, too, almost.

"The reason why I've never been back is because my parents have never gone home . . . and I'm here to find out why. I'm actually here . . . without my parents knowing."

My jaw drops. "You're saying they have no idea you're in Sài Gòn right now."

"No," she says sheepishly. "They think I'm in Singapore."

"Vivi!" I gape at her. "That's . . ." Highly dangerous? Extremely brash?

She sighs. "It sounds *so bad*, but hear me out. That's my mom in the middle, she hates talking about Việt Nam. Every time I try to bring up how we should visit or anything about it, she gets super defensive. And I don't know who the other two women are, but I *think* they're my family."

Family. The word tugs at my chest. "Your mom never told you why she left?"

There are plenty of stories about Vietnamese people in America, gossip about so and so moving across the Pacific years ago, international students marrying abroad, or families upending their entire lives because they scored an immigration visa.

She fidgets with the spoon and avoids my gaze. "Not once. So that's why I'm here without them knowing."

"Maybe there's a reason why your mom left. Sometimes people have to run away, to find something better for themselves."

I wish I could run away sometimes, too. But where would I go?

"She never told me the *reason*, though."

"But . . . what if it's something so horrible that she'd rather keep it to herself?"

She clicks her tongue. "They're my family. *I'm* family. I'm blood related to these people. I deserve to know."

"Blood related doesn't mean . . ." I stop my sentence, seeing her face. "I'm sorry . . . I guess what I'm trying to say is, don't resent your mom too much. You have both of your parents. Some people only have one or neither."

"It's not that black and white, though. I'd rather find out now before, well, they die without telling me."

Memories of Ba and a wave of grief overcome me. She clutches the edges of the photographs in her hands, and I can see tears welling up in the corners of her eyes before she blinks them away. My heart pinches. "I was hoping I'd find these people somehow here . . . but the extent of my abilities is people watching and seeing if any faces match up to the photos—no success there," she says, her shoulders slumped. "I wish I could see them, ask them about my mom, see where she grew up. But my Vietnamese isn't that good, either. I can ask for directions and get by, but I don't think my elementary Vietnamese can help me track down these people without knowing their names.

"Sorry," she sighs. "That was a lot."

I hold the photographs closer, and within the photo of Vivi's mom and the two unnamed women, a sign stares back at me. "This was photographed in front of Chợ Bến Thành."

She brightens. "No way! But . . . where is that?"

"It's this giant market in Sài Gòn," I say. "It's one of our most iconic landmarks, and so the place is always brimming with tourists. Having a stall there is prime real estate because most foreigners don't know how to haggle."

"I can't believe that I have a lead," she says, her eyes still pinned to the photograph and her thumb hovering over the silhouette of her mom. "I have to go to Chợ Bến Thành, then."

"And do what?"

She sighs. "I haven't thought that far yet. Maybe ask everyone at Chợ Bến Thành once I'm there?"

I snort. "Vivi, do you know how many people go in and out of that market every day? That's impossible."

Her face falls. "Oh."

"But," I start again. "They're wearing áo dàis in this photograph. I think I know the cut and patterns of those áo dàis, and if I'm right, I might know someone who can help us point to where your family might be."

She gasps, clutching my hands. Heat rises to my cheeks from the skin-to-skin contact. "*Us?* You would help me? You'd come with? Because, if you say yes, you cannot back out."

Vivi's looking at me as if I'm made of magic, like I have solved the mysteries of life. It feels nice, to bask in that awe; her eyes pinning me and my breath too shy to leave my mouth. But what I know isn't magic, just the life of a girl living in the heart of Sài Gòn.

"Well." I inhale. "How about this, since you're helping me with the submission contest, I'll help you track down the women in the photos. Everyone in Sài Gòn knows someone. We can definitely ask around."

Her face brightens. "Really? You'd do that?"

"Yeah. Why not?" There are many, many reasons why I shouldn't be instigating a wild goose chase around Sài Gòn with a girl I just met, but I owe her something, or at least that's what I tell myself. Plus, I find myself gravitating toward her smile, and the blossoming urge to have her look at me like *that* again.

"What's that thing Americans do with their littlest finger?" I say, holding out my pinkie. "Let's make a deal?"

She laughs and loops her pinkie around mine. I can feel the warmth creeping up my spine.

"Deal," she says, and my heart leaps. "I still can't believe you put all the pieces together from just a building in the background and some áo dàis."

She holds the photographs closer to her chest, almost as if she's afraid they'll disappear. "It's not impossible after all—finding my family in such a big city. I thought it was so silly of me to hope that I'd run into them on the streets. That they'd recognize me, even though we've never met."

Even though Vivi's a girl from across the world and grew up in a city so different from Sài Gòn, she still ended up here, in *my* city, chasing after the phantoms of family and searching for answers. I know that feeling all too well.

Maybe we're more alike than I think.

"We'll go to Chợ Bến Thành together. We'll find them," I say, the promise rolling off my tongue—since when do I make promises? "Somehow or someway, I'm sure you'll meet them."

She smiles, and her dimples make my heart jump. "*And* somehow or someway, we'll win the contest, too. Two miracles can happen at once."

"It's getting late. I'll take you home."

She hesitates. "Take me home?"

I feel the corner of my left lip shaping into a smirk. "Yes. On my motorbike."

She drops her jaw, shocked.

"Is there . . . something wrong with that?"

"No!" she blurts out. "Just . . . I feel like I'm inconveniencing you. You don't have to take me home—I'll figure it out. The internet is free and ever generous."

"Can you please let me take you home before I feel bad about leaving a tourist stranded in the middle of the city?" I know Vivi wouldn't be stranded. Sài Gòn has tons of rideshare apps for tourists and locals alike, but still, a part of me doesn't want to leave her just yet.

She nods, biting her bottom lip. "Thanks."

I help Vivi hop onto my motorbike, our fingers brushing against each other. She fidgets behind me, her books in between us.

"Hold on to me."

"Hold on to you?" She shifts behind me, making my heart race faster. Placing her feet clumsily on the side of the motorbike, she tries angling herself so there's space between us. I bite down a smile.

I lean back into her, closing that space, letting her know that it's okay to touch me. "Yes, or you'll fall off."

Slowly, she inches her arm around my waist, holding on to me firmly.

For someone so bouncy and seemingly brave, she's still shy—like me. "You can just grab my shirt, you know."

"Oh." Jolting, she starts to retract her hands.

"I'm teasing." I hold on to her hands firmly. "This is nice, too."

I turn into the busy traffic of Sài Gòn, joining the sea of motorbikes. We waddle through the crowd during peak rush hour, inching our way through the tide. I glance back at Vivi, a smile on her face as she takes in the city in front of her. The sun settles below the horizon, and kites once again take to the sky. The flying canvases makes me think of Ba, and grief grips me again. But it doesn't feel like it usually does. Instead, I focus on Vivi's warmth behind me, on her arms around my waist, and the loneliness doesn't overwhelm me.

"Wow." Vivi marvels at the kites.

I lean into her. "Do you want to go see the kites?"

"Yes."

I weave through the crowd before turning into a narrow alleyway. Street food vendors selling bánh tráng, cơm tấm and chè mingle among passersby, feeding the people of Sài Gòn.

I can feel Vivi's cheeks smiling against my back.

"Hang on," I say.

Speeding up my motorbike, I swerve us deeper into the vast open field away from the blaring horns and toward the hum of cicadas. Vivi tightens her embrace. My heart is pounding so hard that it's suffocating.

As if on cue, five different paper kites spring from the ground up, riding the wind's current and soaring right above our heads. I speed up again, chasing the kites around us as they dance gracefully across the red-and-orange canvas of the sky. The kites' shades of blue, red, pink, and yellow bleed into the sunset's hues, swirling into a palette that rivals that of traditional Vietnamese paintings. The wind playfully blows on our cheeks and the city's humidity slips away. The earthy scent of the fields tickles my nose—the smell of sweet summer rain from the day before.

She tightens her arms around my waist, sending shivers up my spine. "Lan?"

"Yes?"

"Your Sài Gòn is beautiful."

Chapter Fourteen

VIVI

Almost a day later, and the perfume of orchids still won't leave my clothes, and every time I smell it, I think of Lan—of my arms around her waist, my face against her strong back, and my heart beating so fast I prayed she couldn't hear it.

After making out with Mindy Kim four years ago at freshman year homecoming, I realized that kissing girls is one of the top ten reasons to be alive. I settled on the term *bisexual*, after years of wondering why my face heats up when a girl changes in front of me. Lan makes my heart skip like Mindy, but she also slows it down. I desperately want to see her again.

But does Lan even like girls?

Cindy pounds at my door. "Can you please tell Anh Huy to switch rooms? I missssss you."

I think the C in her name stands for "codependency." "I love you, but no, I don't plan on causing trouble already. What if they email my mom?"

"You know she doesn't check her emails."

"She will be if she sees *Vivi Huỳnh Is Expelled* in the subject line."

"They're not going to *expel* you for switching roommates." She laughs, and gets on my bed. "But, fine, I guess we're going to have to do sleepovers for the entire semester." She brought her pillows and blankets with her.

"You're sleeping here *again*?" Nga groans from her bed that she's currently sharing with five plushies. She has a sheet mask on, a routine she does every night.

"I know," I second Nga's whine. "You can't be that scared of ghosts."

"My room is creepy! It's not my fault I got placed in the only single room and it's cramped and tiny and practically haunted. I swear I heard someone talking the first night."

"People would pay extra for a single," I point out. "And it was probably just noise from the street."

"Definitely the street," Nga adds. "I didn't agree to a triple."

"Me neither."

"All right—can you guys stop making me feel bad?" Cindy pleads as she gets off my twin XL to the makeshift mattress on the floor—blankets and pillows she got from who knows where. "I promise to not snore tonight."

"I don't know if that's physically possible. Unless you don't sleep," Nga comments.

"I do usually have a lot to get done at night."

"She does." I shrug. "A whole folder of fan fictions to get to."

"Leave me alone. I'm not hurting anyone," she grumbles from below.

"I'm not judging."

"You shouldn't be when all you do is stare at Lan from the window and imagine both of you holding hands and skipping through a flower field like a pair of cottagecore sapphics—"

"Cindy!"

"What's this?" Nga appears right next to my bed. "Lan? As in *Lan* from Bánh Mì 98?"

"Gosh, Nga! You literally look like a ghost," Cindy yelps, dropping her phone on her face. "Sorryyyyy. I know it's quiet hours."

Now Nga's on my bed—I guess everyone loves my twin XL. People on the internet were right once again. College is great because it's like summer camp but with unlimited and unauthorized sleepovers.

"You think Lan's cute, huh? It's pretty obvious. You were shaking while talking to her."

I blush, and no words dare escape my mouth.

"She does," Cindy sings. "She most definitely does." She sings again in a crescendo.

"Watch it, Cindy, or else I'm sending you back into that haunted room."

"What are these?" Nga is by my desk now, looking at the pictures I stole from Mom.

"That's my mom in Việt Nam. When she was a girl," I say, relieved someone changed the subject. "I think the other people are my family. I mean, Cindy says we all have the same cheekbones. I brought the photos because . . . I thought I'd try finding family here."

"Your mom was born in Việt Nam?"

I nod at Nga. "Yeah. She rarely speaks of this country, though. My dad, on the other hand, immigrated with my grandpa when he could barely talk, so he doesn't know much, either. The only things I really know about Việt Nam have been through Google and all the weird, traumatic facts taught in US History classes."

"Ugh, AP US History sucked," Cindy scoffs, folding her arms before turning to Nga. "AP US History is this core requirement for 'gifted' American kids to learn about American propaganda. Our teacher, Mr. Smith, would spend twenty minutes on a lesson, then expected us to hand in a full-length project."

Nga winced. "So that class didn't answer your questions, either?"

I nod. "Not a single one. I just wish I knew why my mom immi-grated. It's strange, I'm raised by immigrant parents, but I don't know why they chose to come to California. I don't know if it's a *my family* problem, either, because Cindy's from a family of immigrants, too, and they aren't like that—hiding things about the country they came from."

Nga looks from me to Cindy, shock on her face. "You are? That's so . . . interesting to me, I guess because my family has always been in Việt Nam."

Cindy nods. "Yeah, my family are immigrants—undocumented immigrants to be exact."

"Undocumented . . . ?" Nga cocks her head.

Cindy sighs, taking a finger through her hair. She often does this when the topic of her family immigration comes up, and so I reach out to squeeze my best friend's hand. "My family has no citizenship. They're not Americans, and they can't receive any 'American benefits.' They're paying taxes, but the government pretends they don't exist."

"What? That's just messed up."

I sigh. "And there's nothing they can do."

Cindy continues. "It was hard for me when I was younger. Why on earth would they leave Mexico to go to America? Part of me still doesn't understand. All I know is that they wanted the very best for me and my siblings even if that meant the very worst for them. When they first immigrated, my mamá cried every night. She can't just book a plane ticket back home. She still can't. I don't know how I'd survive that, not being able to see your family for decades."

"And maybe for the rest of her life." Like Mom and her family here. "My mom can easily come back here. She just doesn't want to."

"Your mom has her reasons," Cindy sighs. "Think of it this way: It was hard enough for us to pack up to come here, and we're only here for like four months. Imagine how it must feel to leave without knowing when or if you can come back."

I don't understand how Cindy can tell me that Mom has her reasons when *she* still doesn't understand her own family. But part of me knows she's right. I can't imagine how Mom must have felt leaving by herself.

"That's true." Nga nods. "And from what you told me . . . your mom probably has some things she's just not ready to share yet."

"It's just . . . like look at this photo." I pull the photo of Mom next to the one of my potential aunt and grandma. "Who is she standing next to? Are they even alive?"

"Wooow," Nga drawls. "You're saying you have no idea who these people are. But they're here. In Việt Nam."

"Yeah, and I didn't believe I'd actually be able to find them. I thought it'd be like finding a needle in a haystack, there are *a lot* of Vietnamese people in Sài Gòn. But, um, I asked Lan for help—or rather, she offered—and we're going to try." I mumble the last part real fast, because I still haven't told Cindy, and now she's looking at me like she's about to shake both my shoulders until they fall off.

"No. Way." Cindy jumps from her makeshift bed. "You only told me you ran into her yesterday! *Spill.*"

♡ ♡ ♡

Nga claps her hands together, smiling too. "Lan would know! She sees so many locals every day."

Suddenly, my ringtone blares through the room. "Uh, Viv, your mom's calling."

"Your mom!" Nga squeals. "Maybe I can introduce myself as your roommate—"

"Maybe *not*," Cindy interjects.

I accept the FaceTime call. "Hi! Mom! What's up? I'm in bed."

"Hi, con." Mom greets me with just her nostrils on the screen this time. I've given up trying to teach her where the camera is.

"Chào Cô!" Nga tries peeking over my shoulder, but not before Cindy tackles her.

"Nga, you *really* can't talk," Cindy whisper-begs.

"What was that? Ai nói tiếng Việt vậy?"

"Um."

Shit. Fuck. Shit. Fuck!

"No one's speaking Vietnamese, Mom. I was just, um, watching Vietnamese dramas with Cindy."

"Hey, Cô!" She practically screams, knowing it was her cue to say something. Mom freaks out less when I'm with Cindy.

"Why con do that? Con never watch that before."

"I . . ." Think, Viv, *think*! Mom really always calls at the worst time. "I just miss you and Dad. That's why. You watch Vietnamese dramas all the time at home."

"Oh! Which one is con watching?"

I don't have time to google the trending Vietnamese dramas right now. "Anyway—Mom! Why did you call? Did something happen?"

She waves me off, her palm covering the camera now. "Mommy want to check in! Con doing okay? What did you eat today? You sleep well? You sick?"

"Yes, I had um . . . wonton soup—"

"Again? Con really like wonton soup." Her face is now fully visible, and she's frowning. I hadn't realized I lied about wonton soups so many times. I make a mental note to look up Singaporean cuisine later. Mom is too good at remembering things.

"Yeah! A lot!"

"Mommy will make you wonton soup when you come home. Mommy didn't know you like it so much."

My stomach lurches. The semester has just started, but I miss home already. I miss the smell of bún riêu after school, the taste of fried dumplings and the pandan waffles Mom packs for lunch. What would she say if she knew? Would she kick me out and never cook for me again?

"I miss you," I say. "But I have to sleep now . . . it's late."

"Okay, con, Mommy have a question. Do you know where my photos at?"

I suck in a breath. "What photos?"

She clicks her tongue. "Old photos that Mommy have. I cleaned my closet last night and they are missing!" She passes the phone to my dad, who only nods.

"Hey, Dad." I wave at him. "I don't know what you're talking about, Mom. Maybe you misplaced them somewhere."

"Yeah, con is right. They're very old."

"I'm sure they'll turn up."

Mom's looking directly into the camera now. I feel like her eyeballs are going to see right through me. "Okay, con. Good night. You promise you are good?"

"I'm good, Mommy. Good night!"

"Jesus." Cindy blows a raspberry as I hang up. "You sure your mom isn't some kind of psychic? We were literally just talking about her and then she called."

"Yeah, that was really creepy," Nga adds. "But what's going on, Vivi? You're here illegally?"

I let out an exaggerated sigh. "It's not illegal. They signed the paperwork. Are you sure you want to hear my explanation?"

"Well." Nga joins Cindy on her makeshift bed. "We've got *all* night. And I'd love to hear about Lan, too."

Chapter Fifteen

LAN

"Are you free right now?"

I blink, looking up from the baguettes in my hands to Vivi, and suddenly, I'm all too aware of my pulse and the dampness of my palms. I've spent the last few nights tossing and turning, my heart skipping when I think about her arms around me and how the sky was so pink and red and orange, and how her eyes shone at the sights of this city.

"Vivi—good morning? What are you doing here?"

She smiles. "Can't miss the best bánh mì in Sài Gòn from my favorite food blogger."

My face burns. I hadn't realized how lost in thought I was. I force my mind to shut up, locking away all the fluttering feelings and hot cheeks and fidgety hands that come up when she's near me.

But Vivi has no idea. She's distracted by my notebook. "Have you been writing? Did anything inspire you? How many pages? I'm *sure* we can use what you wrote for the contest—"

She starts rapid firing questions at me, and I struggle to follow, but her eyes are so bright that I can't help but nod along. For the first time since Ba's passing, someone else is excited to hear about my writing. What I'm up to, what I've been thinking about. Maybe I can share the words in this notebook with someone other than Ba.

"Well, there are a lot more words after our little brainstorming session at Café 1975—"

"Brainstorming? We just talked."

"It helped." I shrug. "Or it did *something* because I've been writing nonstop, and . . . I don't hate my words as much anymore." For some reason, I want to tell Vivi everything, to not hold on to the pages so tightly and keep them as backlogged dreams like before. She sparked something, and though I'm still not sure what it is, the words haven't flowed out of me like this for a long, long time.

"Lan, this is *good*," she gushes, holding the leather-bound notebook gingerly in her hands. Unlike the night when we met, I don't feel defensive over Ba's notebook anymore. Instead, I want her to touch it, to run her hands over my inked words, and I want to watch her reaction. It reminds me of when Ba and I would brainstorm in the kitchen, the scent from the boiling vat of Má's phở wafting from the stove.

"This part is about how Sài Gòn comes alive at night? Let's throw in some adjectives, like 'Sài Gòn's vibrant colors emerge when the sky is the deepest blue,' and you're solid."

I burst out laughing. "Okay, that is so corny—I love it."

She grins. "Looks like it's slow right now. Let's go do some field research."

I cock my head. "Field research?"

"I was googling things last night and found this alleyway in District Ten that's basically a giant street food market and thought maybe we could go."

"Sounds like you want a free ride to District Ten so you can go eat."

She rolls her eyes at me, a hand on her hip. "Fine. That was part of the plan, too—but can we go? The colorful flan with tapioca balls looks *so* good I think I'll regret my entire life if I never try it before flying back to California."

I hadn't said *yes* much since Ba's passing, but ever since Vivi crashed into my life—literally—I have been saying yes more than no. Like right now, driving across the city on my motorbike with her arms wrapped around my waist, all I can say is "Yes."

District 10 is one of the innermost districts of Sài Gòn, situated next to District 3 and my home, District 1. There are tall buildings reaching for the blazing sun, motorbikes lining the streets, plastic stools wet from spilled drinks, and street food carts—lots and lots of them.

We veer into an alley, the wandering smell of bánh tráng nướng salting my tongue. Vivi fumbles with her purse before pulling out a photograph. She positions the photo in front of her, eyes narrowing from the alleyway full of street food before us to the picture in her hand.

"Look," she says. "Here's my mom in front of a small street. I just can't wrap my head around that, the fact that I'm where she grew up."

I take the photo from her, my eyes zooming in to the huge smile on the woman's face. "She looks really happy."

"I know. Do you think my mom ate all this street food when she grew up here?"

I nod. "Street food has always been here in Sài Gòn. But I don't know if she ate the same food as the ones in front of us. Food is always changing, and new dishes pop up all the time."

To our right, a girl cracks an egg on top of a bánh tráng and mixes the thin omelet on the rice paper, sprinkling on green onions and sausages before finishing the round pancakes with spreads of mayonnaise and ketchup.

"What is *that*?" Vivi points in the direction of my gaze.

"The bánh tráng nướng? It's a popular street food. It's egg, sausages, and condiments on top of grilled rice paper. I think some people call it a Vietnamese pizza."

"Is this one of the new street food dishes you are talking about?"

"Yup. I think the original bánh tráng nướng was from Da Lat, a city in the Lam Dong Province, north of Sài Gòn, but a modern version made its way to this city. Now it's a quintessential Sài Gòn street food."

"So you're saying, fusion food can be Vietnamese food mixed with Vietnamese food?"

I laugh, finding her innocent question endearing. "There are so many different Vietnamese cuisines. Sài Gòn is considered southern, but there are also northern and central regions. Each one has their own special ingredients in their food."

"That's so cool. I want to try *all* the Vietnamese food. I think I remember you wrote about bánh tráng nướng. It was from a post years ago . . . about the best things to eat after school with friends?"

My heart lurches at Vivi's attentiveness. She does know *A Bánh Mì for Two.* "I can't believe you remember that."

"I always remember the things you write."

My face feels hot. I match my pace with Vivi's, so our hands swing side by side, not quite touching.

We watch another street food seller grind long sugarcane sticks through a hand-powered machine before pouring the juice into plastic pouches. Next to the sugarcane juice is a vendor passing out plates of fresh fruits and chewy tapioca balls piled on colorful flans. Then we see a stall across the street, with heaps and heaps of bánh tráng trộn full of quail eggs, lạp xưởng, fried onions, and the tangy sweet-and-spicy sauce that makes me salivate. More stalls line the winding alleyway on both sides, smoke and chatter floating through the space and twinkling string lights hanging from wall to wall.

"I can't believe you found this. Are you *sure* you don't live here?"

Vivi laughs, tugging me back toward the sugarcane cart. "Lots of research on the internet. I told you I'm all in for this contest, which means finding you some inspiration."

Whatever she's doing . . . is working. This is the heart of Sài Gòn's street food squeezed into a small corner of the city. Suddenly the mundane work I've been doing, the street food I've been selling, seems larger than I had realized. Street food feeds Sài Gòn, and I've been a part of that for so long. I want to write about the sight before me, the people weaving around us, and the food that shapes my home.

We can't decide on what to get, so Vivi and I settle on two pouches of sugarcane, grilled shrimp on sticks, and a plate of bột chiên, or fried rice flour cake.

She pokes a straw through the top of the sugarcane pouch before slurping, her eyes widening as she drinks. "Okay, this is strangely refreshing—it tastes like grass, but also like honey?"

"Vivi, can you write that down? What you just said."

She laughs before shaking her head and pointing to her temple. "Don't worry. I'll remember it. I learned how to describe food from you. There were so many nights when I was drooling over everything you wrote."

"Thanks," I say, the corners of my lips tilting upward again.

She digs into the fried cake with scrambled eggs, serving me first. We both go for the utensils at the same time, our hands brushing again.

"Can I ask you something?"

She nods and tucks a strand of hair behind her ear before biting off a piece of fried cake.

"Why Sài Gòn? We could . . . make up another city to write about—what about somewhere in the States, where you're from?"

She snorts. "Do you know how many people worship NYC or LA? It's so overdone."

I narrow my eyes. "Sài Gòn is overdone, too. What do we have that other people don't? How are we any different?"

"We're not," she says, her eyes locking mine. "I don't think we can ever come up with something so wild and so different that it'll blow the judges away.

"But we don't need to be different." She points to the houses that surround us, their angular structure shaping the alley we're walking through. "Everything looks so imperfect here. I know that's probably not the right word! But people are hanging their laundry on these criss-crossing pipes. There are plants poking out from the walls. I see water bottles being used as plant pots. And the houses! They're so skinny."

"You like the messiness of Sài Gòn? So many tourists complain how it's not clean or—"

"I love it." She smiles sheepishly. "It makes the city feel alive. Like it has a personality. No two things look the same, and I'm seeing something new every time I walk outside."

I find myself looking at my city the way Vivi's looking at it. All this messiness and chaos is mine, my city and my Sài Gòn that I grew up in. She's right. Things are always changing. The same clothes on the rusty pipes will be brought in tonight. Flowers will soon bloom from single-use plastic cups. Even Vivi will be leaving in a couple months.

But that's what makes this city so special, it changes. It lives.

Chapter Sixteen

VIVI

A couple more days pass, and Lan and I settle into a routine: We meet each other at noon to continue tossing ideas back and forth (the norm here, I've learned, is for street food stalls and businesses to take a lunch break or nap). Something changed in Lan after our last visit to the street food alleyway. She's writing a lot more, *sharing* a lot more, and overall seems . . . *happy*. I can see it in how she moves, how her eyebrows have stopped their deep scrunching, and how she lights up when she sees me.

"Random question for research: On a scale of never-visiting-again to must-absolutely-visit, where would you rank Sài Gòn?" I ask Lan, who's busy slicing baguettes open while I scribble down our brainstorming notes.

She dabs at the sweat on her temple. I swallow, hoping my hair is enough to cover the blush creeping to my ears. "Can't rank, 'cause it's the only place I've ever known. I'd love to go outside of this city though, try visiting somewhere else. Live abroad for a while."

"*Really?* You want to leave Sài Gòn? I could live here forever." It's the truth. I don't think I'll ever get tired of Sài Gòn's noise, and I'd rather live in it than drown it out.

"You're only saying that because you're a tourist. Would you want to live in California for the rest of your life?"

I shrug. "It is a big state. But probably not. There's a lot to see outside of California, a lot more to experience. I see your point now."

"But you have beaches . . . Hollywood, the Golden Gate?"

I snort. "I can't tell you how many times people think San Francisco and Los Angeles are right next to each other. And Hollywood is kind of grimy. The real treat is the immigrant-owned restaurants in Southern California and the Bay Area. So much good food. Still, there's something about Sài Gòn that just pulls you in." And once I was pulled, I let this city's fervor seep into me—all the electrifying chaos, the sweltering humidity, and this girl next to me.

She nods. "I can't imagine living without the motorbikes, street food vendors, and Sài Gòn's energy. But Sài Gòn wasn't always like this. All those corner shops and neighborhood marts outside the alley? Those weren't there when I was a kid."

"No way." I try to imagine a Sài Gòn from the past, and who knows, maybe the buildings I've been looking at didn't exist when Mom was here. Maybe these skyscrapers would be as new to Mom as they are to me. Maybe the place she used to call home . . . no longer looks like home.

"See that super-tall building ahead?" Lan continues. "That's Landmark 81. It's the highest building in Việt Nam. It was built in 2015."

"That's so recent." And definitely way after my parents left. "But to me, Landmark 81 feels like it's always been part of Sài Gòn. Wherever you stand in this city, you can always see it."

"It's crazy to watch the city change."

"My parents . . . they're refugees." I avoid her gaze, unsure of how to approach the word—the topic. "I really don't know much about what it was like for them living here—leaving here. We've never had a long talk about their lives before California. All I know is that my dad's father, or my grandpa, left soon after the war ended when my dad was only three. He grew up in Little Saigon like me. My mom immigrated in the nineties, though. I want to know why they left, especially my mom."

"Sometimes it's not easy and there aren't black-and-white answers," she says, looking at the dangling mess of electrical wires above us, bird nests poking through. There's a hint of sadness to her tone, and I wonder if Lan ever thinks about leaving this city. "I wasn't born yet, but everyone told me how hard it was back then."

"I know, but why run away?" Across an entire ocean, too, no less.

"Maybe that's all they knew, all they could do: Run to survive. I'm from a family of immigrants, too. My great-grandma is người Hoa."

Confused, I cock an eyebrow. I didn't know that there were other types of Vietnamese people. "Người Hoa?"

Lan nods. "Vietnamese people who are ethnically Chinese. My great-grandma emigrated from China and built our family with my great-grandpa, who's Vietnamese. My dad grew up speaking Vietnamese and practicing Vietnamese culture in Sài Gòn. Most Người Hoa, though, are from Chợ Lớn, our Chinatown."

"I never knew that!" A rush of adrenaline courses through my body. This is exactly what I wanted from this trip. Everything my parents never told me.

What would Mom think?

"The Kinh group is the dominant ethnicity of this country, but there's Tày, H'Mông, Chăm, Lào, and many more. Some still practice their traditions and culture, but for me, I've always called myself Vietnamese."

"Wow." I watch her in awe, how she moves with such precision while dressing bánh mìs and talking to me. I want to bottle up this moment between us—two girls on the streets under the beating sun, learning . . . and unlearning. "For the longest time, I didn't know how to label myself. Still don't."

"What do you mean?"

"Growing up in the States, even though I was surrounded by other Vietnamese people in Little Saigon, I always felt out of place. Walking outside of my own bubble was an experience . . . I didn't know the world could be so *white*. I thought that maybe I wasn't American enough and that my family would never be accepted despite being there for so long—despite America literally being my home."

"But does that matter?" She turns toward me, her eyes firmly locked on mine, and I almost forget her question.

"What do you mean?" I breathe out, feeling my cheeks warming.

She shrugs, going back to the baguette in her hands. "Maybe it's okay to not be anything. To not have to label yourself as anything. You can be *both* Vietnamese and American."

It hadn't occurred to me that I could be both before. That I shouldn't force myself to fit into one definition of what it means to be Vietnamese, or what being an American looks like. It feels validating to know I shouldn't—can't—be put in a box, that it's okay to float in this in-betweenness . . . to be everything at once. I don't have to compromise my identity. I can be so many different things.

"You're right. Thanks, Lan."

The corners of her mouth turn upward, and she smiles brightly, eclipsing the sun's rays. Her braid sways with the wind, the strands of hair framing her sun-kissed cheeks. Half of me wants to reach toward her, to tuck in those strands behind her ear, and to run my fingers through her soft hair.

"I'm just glad I could help," she says.

It's past my lunch break now, and I know Cindy's going to blow up my phone if I don't come back to the dormitory soon. Still, I find myself dragging my own feet, not wanting to tear myself from her. "I have to head back now, but I'll . . . see you tomorrow?"

She nods. "Don't forget we're going to Chợ Bến Thành tomorrow!"

"I can't wait!" I wave at her as I cross the street—with much more confidence than my first day here.

The dormitory looks more homey now than it did when I first arrived, too. Books, backpacks, and someone's consoles are strewn on the tables in the living room. The ceiling fan buzzes from above, struggling to cast away the heavy air even with the windows open.

But instead of going up the stairs, I venture into Bà Hai's kitchen, following the smell of bún hò huế. I spot the giant vat of soup immediately, the spices and pork simmering inside.

"What are you doing, Vivi?"

I jump, not fully registering the small elderly lady crouching behind tall kitchen shelves. "Hi, Bà Hai! Sorry—I know you don't like people coming in here. The bún hò huế just smells so good." I trail off, realizing how awkward I sound.

She blinks, then cackles, her laugh vibrating through the tight space and rattling the cabinets full of spices. "Don't be silly, you all are more than welcome here. Although I do tend to be cranky if anyone touches my food. Only I can make it taste good."

My nerves loosen with her laugh. Sometimes I wonder about the people that raised my parents. Some nights, I find Dad in the kitchen alone at 3:00 a.m., fumbling through old photographs of his parents, who I never got to meet. Mom's family . . . I hope Lan and I can find them, but still, it feels impossible.

Bà Hai motions for me to come near her, and I tiptoe toward the kitchen counter, which has been invaded by every single brand of fish sauce, and of course, condensed milk. "Here." She presses a colorful cup into my hand. "Go on, try it. Let me know how it tastes."

I eye the dessert curiously, noting the red bean paste at the bottom of the cup. "Is this chè?"

"Yes, it is!" She beams, her face looking *proud.* "It's chè ba màu. It has three layers: red beans on the bottom, mung bean in the middle, and the top is green pandan jelly with coconut milk and shaved ice."

Taking my spoon, I scoop up all the different layers at once, bringing the red beans, mung beans, pandan jelly, coconut milk, and shaved ice to my mouth. My mind explodes with vibrant colors, the sweetness tingling my tongue. "This tastes just like halo-halo!" There's a mom-and-pop Filipino restaurant near my house in Little Saigon where Cindy and I would order halo-halo almost every day after school.

Bà Hai grins, the wrinkles on her face curving upward. "Unlike halo-halo, there's no ube. It's all in the rich flavor of the mung beans."

"It's really fascinating how similar some foods are between different cultures," I comment, still digging through my chè ba màu.

"You're really passionate about food, aren't you?"

I blush. Maybe I've been thinking too much about food lately because of Lan. *Definitely* because of Lan.

"Oh right," Bà Hai says while reaching for a pot. I step forward to help, but she swats my arm away. "How are you and Lan getting along? Her and her mother make great bánh mì. I always cater from their business."

My jaw goes slack. "You were watching me?" If there's one thing about older Vietnamese women, it's that they always know what's going on.

Bà Hai scoffs, throwing her arms in the air. "Of course! Have to make sure my students are staying clear of trouble."

I lean farther into the countertop, my hands wandering to the nearest bottles of spices—they'll reach for anything when I'm nervous.

"Lan is great. We're hanging out a lot together because . . . well, I'm helping her with something"—that sounds super shady—"but she's showing me all these cool things about the city." I feel myself instinctively smiling, like I always do when I think of her. "I really like being around her."

Bà Hai ruffles my hair and swats me away from the countertop, prying the bottles from my hands. "Be a good friend to her. That girl works the hardest."

Bà Hai doesn't need to tell me twice. I know Lan works the hardest, I know she's always trying her best. So with a nod, I say, "I will."

"Here, take these lychees for yourself, I just cut them up." Even with my protests, Bà Hai presses the plate of fruits into my hand and ushers me out of the kitchen.

The plump fruits stare back at me, their juice glistening under the hallway light, and suddenly, I see Mom's face in the shape of the plate. I see her skinning each lychee with care, fingers pressed on the husk and peeling it away to reveal the white flesh. I see Mom smiling, her face full of warmth as she gestures for me.

But the memory fades, and I'm reminded of all my lies and what's left unsaid between us.

Chapter Seventeen

LAN

Chợ Bến Thành, the largest market in Sài Gòn, welcomes me and Vivi with its imposing clock tower. Even among Sài Gòn's busy streets and tall business towers, Chợ Bến Thành stands out with its beige paint and French architecture. But the best part is inside: A giant marketplace houses Sài Gòn's bustling stalls full of food and people.

"This is it. The place from my mom's photo," Vivi says beside me. "I can't believe I'm standing here, right where she was years ago. It feels . . . weird."

I don't say anything, only nod. Is this how Americans are? Vietnamese people are blunt. We tell each other the first thing that comes across our minds. My thoughts wander back to when she told me about her grand plan to hide her trip to Việt Nam from her parents and find the people in the photographs on her own. I found it unfathomable, and I still do, because wouldn't it be easier to just . . . ask? Do Vivi and her mom not communicate with each other? Why go through the wild goose chase when they can just *talk*? Then again, it's not like

I've been doing a whole lot of talking with Má either. Plus, I'd told Vivi I'd help, and I don't plan on breaking that promise.

I help Vivi hop off the motorbike, her ponytails kissing my cheeks. She dusts off her skirt and, without warning, takes my hand again and tugs us both out of the parking lot and toward the colorful market.

My heart skips, my eyes zeroing in on our clasped hands, and I suddenly feel all too aware of my palms slicked with sweat.

"Calm down! The market isn't going anywhere," I say, but I speed up my pace to match Vivi's. "I know where to find the person we're looking for. She'll still be here, don't worry!"

Vivi shakes her head. "That's not what I'm worried about. You didn't think this entire excursion would only be about me, did you?"

I furrow my brows. "What? We agreed to come here to see if anyone knows your family—"

"We can't miss our chance for more research! Come on, we have competition." She draws us closer to the heart of the market and into the surging wave of the crowd.

I feel light on my feet with Vivi next to me, and my mind replaying what she said. Part of me is touched that she planned this day for *both* of us, that she thinks of me. But another part of me wonders if it's because she's not ready to find out about her family yet. I know how that feels. It's how I feel about the books Ba left me. When you're so close to the answer, you almost don't want to keep going because it's safer to stay in the dark. Because maybe knowing is the scariest part.

We continue to dodge people pouring in from every direction— vendors carrying goods to their stalls, customers haggling with shop-keepers. "This place is just amazing," Vivi breathes.

"You don't have anything like this in the States?"

She drags us toward a jewelry vendor. "We do. We have Phước Lộc Thọ, or Asian Garden Mall. They have small vendors like this inside and even performances sometimes. They have night markets, too, kind of like street food in a parking lot, but it's nothing like this. Like being right here in Việt Nam."

"Well, Phước Lộc Thọ probably doesn't have a live fish tank."

She makes a face and pinches her nose at the salty smell of fish wafting through the air. "Nope. They do not butcher the fish's head off right in front of people, either."

I shrug. "What's that thing you say? That whatever happens around us is what makes Sài Gòn so special?"

She laughs, her ears red and exposed by the pigtails on her head. "You've been listening."

"*And* I have it written down. It's a good line."

She beams. "Then let's find more things to write about!"

I follow Vivi's trail while she busies herself with investigating every single vendor, curiously sweeping her eyes over all the colors and shapes in front of us. I clear my throat, aware that our hands are almost touching again. "Are you having a great time?"

"Of course—oh!" She squeals excitedly and points to a row of embroidered blankets before holding up one with a tiger and taking my hand, running my fingers over the silk—her hand on top of mine. "Isn't it so soft?" She coos.

The fabric is soft, much softer than anything I own, but Vivi's fingers are softer. They're also searing into my skin. I yank my hand away quickly as my heartbeat hammers throughout my body and my throat. Turning away to hide my flustered face, I nod. "Yes, you should buy it."

"But do you like the pattern?"

"The tiger looks lovely, but . . ." My eyes trail to another blanket, this one embroidered with stars. "This one reminds me of Sài Gòn on a clear night, when you can see the constellations and the moon."

Her gaze follows mine. "That one? You like the night sky?"

Flustered, I shake my head. "No, pick what *you* like."

Still, she picks the starry blanket and tucks it under her arm, ready to dig for her purse. "I'm choosing this one, and I'm buying it for the memories."

"Memories?"

Sticking out her tongue at me, she opens her wallet to pay for the fabric. "Yeah, to commemorate today. Every time I look at it, I'll be instantly reminded of when we went to Chợ Bến Thành together."

I avoid her eyes, planting them on the grimy market floor. The millions of imagined butterflies swarm my stomach as my pulse quickens. "Back to research." I try to not think about her skin on mine again. "What can we write about?"

"Don't you see it, Lan?"

"What? It's just a market. Aside from, I don't know, the live fish we talked about, it's just like any other indoor marketplace."

"It's not!" she protests, extending her arm to point at various shops. "Even though this place can be smelly and loud, it's like its own tiny world. To you, these sounds and smells are home, so you don't find it odd. To me, it's new. It's different. It's beautiful."

I look at the girl next to me, bewildered by the world around her. I think of Vivi's Asian Garden Mall in Little Saigon and wonder how different it is from my own city. Do people sell different things? Do they haggle like us? Does Little Saigon feel like home to her?

Nodding, I take in her words, my eyes observing the market in a new light. Fresh vegetables cultivated by calloused hands. Splashing fishes and eels and clams caught by fishermen whose livelihoods depend on the sea, who always brave the water no matter the storm. Silk fabric sewn intricately by women who do it all for their families. Food chopped, cooked, and served in front of customers by people who should be world-class chefs.

"Write the Sài Gòn that you see, that you experience. Write from *your* eyes, Lan."

I swallow a lump in my throat, Vivi's words tugging at my chest, but it doesn't feel heavy. Rather, my body feels light. Like something has been unlocked. "Thank you, Vivi. I don't know what I'd do without you." Maybe I wouldn't have entered the contest. Maybe I would never have found out about it, if she had never sent it to me.

There are so many people around, but I only see Vivi. Only her eyes locking on mine, their sincerity never wavering.

"Lan?" someone calls from behind us, making me jump. A stout lady peers at us, carrying a coconut in one arm and a stack of fabric in the other.

I smile, folding my arms and offering a slight bow to Cô Ngân. Vivi does the same. "Chào Cô, how are you?"

"Lan! I haven't seen you in so long. Are you well? Have you eaten?"

Another smile tugs at my lips at her question. For Vietnamese people, asking if someone has eaten is how to say *I love you*.

"Yes, Cô, thanks for asking," I say.

"Who is this?" Vivi whispers to me.

"This is the person I was telling you about. The owner of the áo dài store in this market."

She swallows. "Oh. I guess it's time . . . to ask."

My shoulders slump, and a sinking feeling settles in my chest. I wish I could cheer her up, instill the same confidence she's been giving me. "Hey, it's okay. You don't have to do this. We can always . . . leave."

But it comes out wrong, because that's the only thing I know: to avoid, to run away.

Vivi shakes her head. "I have to know."

I nod, already knowing she'd say that. "Cô." I turn back to Cô Ngân. "I hate to bother you, but do you have some time?"

Cô Ngân returns my smile. "Of course! Anything for you, Lan. And you can introduce me to your friend, too!"

Vivi shifts uncomfortably beside me. I inhale deep and say, "This is Vivi, and um, we have something to ask you—"

"Vivi!" Cô Ngân turns to Vivi, both her hands fully on Vivi's shoulders now. "This is the first time I'm meeting Lan's friend." I blush at that comment. "Why do you look so sickly? Did you eat? Do you want food?"

Vivi, bewildered by Cô Ngân's onslaught, bursts out laughing. "Thank you, Cô! But I'm fine. I was just . . . worried about inconveniencing you."

It's a lie, I know it. But still, it warms me—seeing how Vivi lights up because of Cô Ngân.

"Nonsense. Any friend of Lan's is a friend of mine. Now, why don't we go to my shop and you can tell me what you need?"

Arriving at Ngân Fabrics, Cô Ngân drops her coconut on a bamboo mat and gets up to hang her new fabrics on the streamers. Mannequins dressed in áo dàis of all colors and designs surround us.

I'm about to open my mouth to explain again when Cô Ngân interrupts. "Before I help you girls with whatever you need, can I ask for a favor from you, Vivi?"

Vivi blinks, turning to me before answering. "*Me?* Yes! Of course. Tell me what you want me to do, Cô."

"You're adorable." Cô Ngân pinches Vivi's cheeks and shoves a pile of áo dài into her arms. "Here, try these on. I want you to model for me."

Vivi's cheeks flare red. "Um, okay. Are you sure this is okay?" She turns toward me again. I just shrug. Vietnamese women do what Vietnamese women want, and there's no stopping them.

I push her toward the dressing room, my palm flat against her back. "Just humor her," I say, hoping this moment will take Vivi's mind off thinking about her mom, even if just for a bit.

Vivi walks toward the makeshift dressing room in the corner constructed from curtains hanging down, an ingenious idea that vendors use when selling within indoor markets like this. I hear the sound of her clothes shuffling around and blush, looking away to distract myself.

"Lan?" Vivi pipes up. "Can you help me? I can't reach the zipper."

I excuse myself from Cô Ngân and stop outside the curtain, unsure of what to do. "Do you want me to come inside?"

"Yes."

I peer inside the curtain and blush. Vivi's back is exposed to me, her skin glowing against the darkness of the dressing room. The searing heat meets my fingers once again. I'm losing my mind over this simple task.

At last, the zipper works.

I suck in my breath, too scared to let her hear the way she's making me feel. "Is it too tight?"

She shakes her head. "Nope. It's perfect."

"Let me see!" Cô Ngân insists from outside.

I walk out, giving Vivi time to gather herself. She peeks under the curtain and steps out in a pale lavender áo dài with lotus flowers flowing on her skirt, shimmering beneath the fluorescent light. The lace collar complements her small neck, and the white pants float with her every move. A loud exhale escapes me, and my jaw goes slack as I bring a palm up to cover the blush blooming across my face. I can feel my heart in my chest, my arms, my fingers, and my stomach. Vivi looks like she just stepped out of a painting.

"Beautiful! You should model for these dresses!" Cô Ngân exclaims.

She hesitates, shyly crossing her arms over her chest. "I'm not sure if I'm that pretty . . ."

"Oh, hush, you are. Isn't that right, Lan?"

I blink, nodding slowly. "Yes, Vivi's really pretty."

At my comment, Vivi ducks her head under the curtain again, mumbling something between the lines of "thank you" and "oh my God." She emerges again minutes later, flustered and *absolutely over* what just happened.

"So, what did you girls need?" Cô Ngân asks, completely oblivious to why Vivi and I are sitting with a gap between us. My cheeks are still hot, and as I peek at her, I can see her pink ears, too.

Vivi's fingers tremble slightly as she places the photograph of her mom and her family standing in front of Chợ Bến Thành on the bamboo mat. But unlike earlier, she seems more at ease now. More confident. "Lan told me you might know who these people are."

Cô Ngân studies the photo. "Oh yes! I remember them. This girl"— she points to Vivi's mom—"her name's Hoa, isn't it?"

Vivi gasps. "Yes! So you know who they are."

"That's Hoa, her sister, and her mom. I used to see them every day. Until Hoa up and went to America." Cô Ngân smiles sadly. "At least that's what the neighborhood gossips say, little Hoa went to the States all by herself."

Vivi avoids Cô Ngân's gaze, and I just watch them while fidgeting with the hem of my shirt . . . unsure of what to say. Still, I scoot closer to Vivi before placing a hand over hers. I don't know why, but I just know that if I were her, I'd want someone to comfort me in this moment.

"But I don't blame Hoa." Cô Ngân speaks again. "Maybe she found something better for herself. Everyone knows how hard it was back then."

Vivi swallows. "What do you mean?"

Cô Ngân looks at her sadly. "You're Vietnamese American, aren't you?"

Vivi immediately shrinks into herself at that question. I find myself getting restless, wanting to protect her.

"It's okay that you don't know," Cô Ngân says. "A lot of younger kids still don't. But what do you think happens when a war is over? Fighting is easy. Living is hard. And how do you live, or hold on to that hope of living, when you've seen your country torn apart? When you don't know when life will look up again? It was so, so tough for everyone. And when all you know is harshness, you want to run away from it, too."

"I . . . *knew* that." Vivi breathes out. "I guess more than most kids?

I've read a lot about Việt Nam, thanks to Lan." My heart leaps again. "But I . . . never thought about my family and how they went through all the terrible stuff the Wikipedia pages talk about. It's easy to read about the numbers of people dying and what happened when it's just dry facts, but much harder to imagine the people you know experiencing the same things."

But Vivi isn't the only one feeling that way. Even I, a girl who grew up here in Sài Gòn, sometimes find it hard to believe that such a beautiful city went through hell.

Cô Ngân's eyes soften. "As long as you know, that is good enough. But for these people . . ."

Vivi's face falls. "So we can't find them after all."

I squeeze her hand again, feeling her gaze on me. "Just listen, Cô's about to say something."

She returns to the photo, her eyebrows still scrunched. "Though I don't see them anymore, I think someone I know may have an idea. Lan, you know the uncle who sells cơm tấm—the one that was friends with your dad?"

My chest squeezes tight at the mention of Ba, except not as tight as it used to. I nod. "Bác Tuấn."

"Yes, ask Bác Tuấn about these people. He might know them. He went to school with the daughters in the photo."

Vivi's face brightens immediately, and she scoops the photo back into her hands, cradling it against her chest. "Thank you, Cô. You don't know how much you've helped me."

I face Vivi, warmth fluttering through my body at her smile. Still, I'm relieved my hunch was right. Everyone in Sài Gòn really knows *someone*.

She looks at me, really looks at me, and I find myself wanting to keep helping her. To keep sitting next to her just like this, giving her comfort if she needs me.

Chapter Eighteen

VIVI

Lan and I continue wandering through Chợ Bến Thành, my mind pre-occupied with Mom and the women in the photograph. Somehow and somewhere along the way, Sài Gòn stopped being a study abroad fluke, a secret I'd pocket forever once I boarded my return flight. I'm really on my way to unfolding Mom's history. *My* history.

While I'm lost in thought, my hand accidentally brushes against Lan's, causing my stomach to do its silly little flip for the umpteenth time today. My heart, as always, runs miles whenever I'm near her. Whenever the lightest touch of her skin meets mine. Everything she says makes my thoughts blurry.

Vivi's really pretty.

"Are you okay?" Lan asks, concerns dripping from her voice. Her eyes scan my body, and as a response, I stiffen immediately. I bite my cheek, and my ears heat up again as I remember what just happened. How her fingers felt on my exposed back.

I nod, eyes covered by the hair falling on my face.

She reaches to tuck them away, her lips parting. The scent of orchids overwhelms me. "Here, Cô Ngân wanted to give you this."

My jaw drops at the perfectly packaged áo dài I just tried on. "The purple dress? You're kidding. I can't take this."

Lan only rolls her eyes and presses the bundle into my arms again. "It's not your choice. If you return the áo dài, you'll offend her." Seeing my shocked face, she bursts out laughing. "I'm kidding. But don't return it. Or else she'll think that you find it ugly."

"I would never! After what she's just done for me—"

My phone vibrates, and of course, it's a call from Mom. I can't ignore it, or else she'd freak and call me twenty more times before trying the fake number of my Singapore study abroad program and finding out . . . I've been lying.

"Hey, Mom! How are you?"

"Vivi? What are you doing right now?"

Beside me, Lan lingers, eyes looking past me. My stomach recoils. Today was supposed to be just me and her, and I was looking forward to it all this time. Why do I feel like every time I think of Mom, I summon her?

"I'm—um—having lunch. It's really loud. Can I call you back?" I manage to say back.

"What are you eating?"

A woman screams to my right, causing Lan to whip her head around. "Chết Cha!"

"What was that?"

"Nothing! Cindy just loves watching Vietnamese dramas. She's doing it again!" I mentally apologize to Cindy and thank her for being the only person I can throw under the bus for almost anything.

The lines on Lan's forehead deepen. She must think I'm going off the rails. I've already told Lan about *why* I'm not letting Mom know, but it still doesn't help the fact that I look . . . ungrateful, and just straight up stupid for lying to my mom on the phone with Lan next to me.

"Well, Mommy just wants to check in on you. Con eating okay? Sleeping okay? Are you sick?" Mom calls me every day and asks the same questions, even though she knows I can fend for myself.

"No, no." I try covering the phone and speak louder to drown out the Vietnamese being thrown in every direction. "I'm fine. Promise."

"Mommy miss you."

My chest tightens. Most of the time, I brush her off when she says she misses me. But this time, I wish I could tell her I *do* miss her, that I've been thinking of Mom ever since arriving in Sài Gòn, and that all I can do is imagine her life here and everything she hasn't told me.

But I can't, so instead I say, "Con nhớ mẹ. I miss watching K-dramas with you and reading next to you. Or just going grocery shopping. But I miss your food the most."

"Come home soon, con. Mommy thương con."

"I love you, too, Mom."

Mom never says "love" in English. Instead, she says *thương*—the first Vietnamese word I ever learned. *Thương* doesn't just mean love, it's a special kind of love, and the meaning floats between "sacrificial love" and "unconditional love."

I wonder if Mom will ever say *thương* to me again if she finds out about this trip.

A soft hand lands on my shoulder. "That went well. Your mom didn't find out."

I snort. "Well, someone screaming 'motherfucker!' in Vietnamese almost tipped her off."

She laughs. "That's just how it is here. Chaos everywhere."

"Do you find it hard to talk about family sometimes?" I blurt out, still reeling from the phone call. "Or find it so hard to know what to say to them?"

Lan nods. "I . . . never know what to talk about with my mom. All I know how to do is work hard, be there for her, and hope that's enough."

My heart feels heavy for Lan. I *don't* know how that feels: to have to take care of someone you love, to work yourself to the bone for your family. "Sometimes, I wish I was brave enough to tell my mom what I want—to not back down when I sense that she's angry with me. To make her understand how I feel, too. You always know what to do, Lan. You always know how to be a good daughter. I don't."

Lan stays quiet, her gaze avoiding mine.

"Today was the first time I've been back since my dad . . . passed." She speaks again, her eyes misty. "It's been years, and yet I couldn't step foot into this market again until now. I guess in my head, I thought that if I didn't come back, then maybe the memories of him would still be alive—that the last thing I'd remember about this place would be that I shared it with him." She heaves the last part out with a sigh. As if it was a secret that she kept to herself.

"I'm not brave, Vivi," she continues. "*You* made me brave somehow. With you here, I felt less . . . alone. And for some reason, I felt the same today as I did years ago with my dad: *happy*."

A gnawing feeling claws up my chest, and I try to force it down along with the lump in my throat. All this time, I've been going on about how Mom can't understand me without even thinking of Lan and her grief over her dad. I almost think about living without Mom—almost, because I can't. Can't imagine not hearing her nagging through the phone.

"What . . . happened four years ago, Lan? Only if you want to tell me."

Lan's eyes meet mine, and because we're mere inches apart, I can see the sadness eclipsing her irises. Her throat bobbles, and without knowing if it's a boundary I can cross, I reach for her arm and pull her into me. Her cheek meets the crook of my neck, and she sniffles faintly against my ear.

"He was helping my mom deliver a catering order, but on the way back, he had a stroke. His health was already deteriorating, but he kept it all from us. Someone from the hospital called us that night."

"I'm sorry, Lan." Sniffles turn into tears, but I welcome them. "He was taken from you too soon. I'm sorry you've had to take care of your mom all alone. It must have been hard, hasn't it?"

"Yeah." The tears roll down her cheeks, each droplet larger than the last. "It's been really, really, really hard."

"I'm—I'm sorry," I choke out. "For dragging you here and being so stupid and making this whole day about me."

She shakes her head, smiling sadly as she wipes away the tears. "No. It felt like I was doing something I like. Not working the bánh mì stall, not running errands, not sitting somewhere and trying to write. But exploring, trying new things, *having fun*. Being at Chợ Bến Thành helps me see Sài Gòn in a new light. Does that sound weird?"

"No, it doesn't. I think it sounds like you really, really love this city." To love your own home, I've realized, is something so special, and to think I could help Lan feels like a dream.

She nods. "I do."

The crowd in the market has thinned out, yet Lan still holds on to my hand tightly as if I might let go of her. Has she noticed the way our palms feel against each other, too? The way I'm so flustered just because of her touch?

A loud boom shakes through Chợ Bến Thành.

I jump. "What was that?"

She laughs. "Probably rain."

Rain? Rain doesn't make this kind of sound.

She cocks her head. "What? Doesn't it rain everywhere?"

"I'm from California. It's a desert. You can fry an egg on the pavement in the summer there," I say defensively.

From inside the market, we watch the torrential downpour. There's something intimate about watching the rain with Lan. Just like the rain, what started as an off-chance meeting turned into a summer rain flooding my every thought.

Water pools around our feet as we near the entrance, our sandals sloshing through puddle after puddle. To say that it's raining is an understatement. Rain in Southern California usually sounds like *pit-pat*. This rain is just buckets pouring from the sky, splashing onto our clothes and shoes and hair and faces.

"It's monsoon season."

It's *what* season? I gape at her nonchalance. "How on earth are we going to make it home?"

Her eyes twinkling with mischief—a side I haven't fully seen yet—she points at the water. "We can swim through it."

"Did you just say *swim*?" I give her an incredulous look.

"Yeah, wait here for me to get the motorbike."

Lan returns moments later. Sài Gòn is practically submerged underwater now, brown waves flooding the streets and almost reaching up to our knees. Lan tosses me a raincoat from the motorbike's trunk and orders me to put it on. The yellow poncho makes me look ridiculous. "Do I have to wear this?"

"Yes, unless you want to get sick."

I pick at the poncho, swaying back and forth to check myself. I look like a Teletubby. "Can't we just use an umbrella?"

"No!" She gives me her hand. "That's dangerous. Hop on."

I take her hand, my skin burning against the coolness of the rain as our arms brush past each other.

"Hold on to me tighter this time. Tighter than when we saw the kites."

Blushing, I wrap my arms around her, and instead of simply holding on, I'm embracing her—embracing the girl who makes me burn. She maneuvers with her legs through the flood, mumbling sorry whenever water splashes onto my clothes. Soon, we reach an intersection and join the other motorbikes swimming through the current, the murky water dragging plastic bags and leftover food and plastic chairs. The rain beats down on our backs and I press closer to her, wishing to shield her from the stinging shower that threatens the softness of her skin. Around us, people tread water with their motorbikes, but the chaos of the city only intensifies. Some are rushing home, swerving past us without honking and not caring about who they'd bump into.

"Ouch!" I yelp. Something just cut me and it stings.

Lan whips her head around. "Are you okay?"

My leg throbs in pain, and a line of red trickles down my foot and inks my white socks. "Yeah, I think—I think something scratched my leg. I'm okay though, just keep going."

Lan says nothing and we continue, swimming through the currents while I tighten my embrace. She leads us onto an unfamiliar road and stops in front of a pharmacy. "Here, let me help you get down."

"Lan—"

Wrapping me in her arms, she gathers my shoulders and helps me wobble to the front steps of the pharmacy. "You're not fine. I felt you hissing in pain from behind me. It'll get infected if we don't treat it."

She lowers me onto the stoop by the storefront, wiping rainwater from my knees. "Wait here," she orders, and heads for the pharmacy's counter.

I nod, fidgeting with my hands and the sloppiness of my socks and shoes. Lan comes back carrying a first aid kit. Dropping to her knees, she wipes water off my legs with a towel. Finding it hard to stay still, I grit my teeth.

"Relax, I'm not going to hurt you."

"I know," I whisper. I know that she wouldn't. Ever.

She holds my knees gingerly, tenderly, brushing feather-light touches on my goose bumps, kissing it all with her fingers. The pain dissipates, replaced by the searing heat of skin to skin—thundering heartbeats matching the drums of the monsoon. She locates the slit on my leg and gently rubs the disinfectant on it. The medicine stings, and I tighten my jaw. Lan intertwines her left hand with my right one, smoothing the lines of my palm as she works on my leg with her other hand. Outside, the thunderstorm pounds on the roof, joining the chorus of motorbikes honking and trees howling with the wind.

She places the bandage over my cut, pausing before letting her touch fall from my skin.

Chapter Nineteen

LAN

Vivi and I rode home in silence. Even the brisk rain couldn't extinguish the burning inside my chest. As I reluctantly watched her back disappear behind the dormitory doors, I thought about the way our hands touched, the way my fingers lingered on her back, and the way she hung on to me.

I slip inside the house, careful not to kick Triết while tiptoeing past the living room. I'm dripping wet from head to toe, my clothes leaving puddles on the floor behind me. Má snores softly from her room, the ceiling fan whirring above. Triết, to his credit, doesn't snore. He's sprawled across the bamboo mattress in the living room with two pillows tucked under his arm and a stack of engineering books piled next to his head. In the dark, I bump into the living room table and groan.

"You're back?" Triết mumbles, half-asleep. He rubs his eyes and yawns, making me jump.

"Shh, you'll wake Má up!" I whisper-yell.

He sits up and clears a space on the mattress for me to sit down. "Relax. She's not going to yell at you. You're grown."

I shove the pile of textbooks onto the floor, grimacing at its weight, and sit down. Outside, the thunder and rain drown out all the sounds of Sài Gòn. "Not that . . . I just don't want to wake her up. She needs rest."

He gives me an incredulous look and bursts out laughing. "Is that what you tell yourself? It's not because you don't want her to find out about your girlfriend?"

"*Girlfriend?*" I scoff.

He slides back down onto his back and shoves me away with one leg. Offended, I slap his arm.

"Go to bed. I don't need your negative energy right now. I have an exam tomorrow," he says.

"Here's some good energy," I say, making rippled waves with my arms pointing at him. "Feel it yet?"

He pretends to catch the nonexistent energy waves. "Sure. You can tell me all about your *date* tomorrow."

I roll my eyes. "Who says that I'll tell you?"

"Then who else are you going to talk to about it?"

I smack his arm again, earning a hiss from him. "I'm going to sleep. Good luck tomorrow."

"Good night, little sister!"

Plopping onto my own mattress, I look up at the ceiling above my bed. Glow-in-the-dark stars and constellations stare back at me. They're cheap stickers, a gift from Ba. Má thought they were ugly, but I was so insistent that she gave in. The stars still glow brightly even though years have passed, as if they're trying to remind me of him. We'd lie in this room together just like this, counting stars until I fell asleep.

Look at the stars, con. Can you see Bắc Đẩu thất tinh?

I'd nod at his words, pointing out the shape of the Big Dipper. *It looks like a spoon.*

He'd laugh. *Do you see how Đại Hùng tinh and Tiểu Hùng tinh are next to each other?*

I'd nod, noting the Big and Little Dipper side by side. *Why are they always together?*

Because, con à, you always need someone by your side. But you see the Big Dipper? That's me. Con, you're my Little Dipper. Ba will always be with you.

A heavy weight settles on my heart. I twist and turn and avert my eyes from the ceiling until they land on the pile of picture books that Ba gave me. They've been collecting dust in this closet. I turn away from the books and face the wall instead. It's better not to think about them right now. I need to sleep.

Or not.

Frustrated with myself, I get up and walk toward the books. I take the first one, a story about a girl magically transported into a world with a talking cat and magical cards. I flip the cover open, and an envelope falls out of it. *To Lan*, it reads.

I wrinkle my eyebrows and pry the envelope open, smoothing my hand over a birthday letter written by Ba a long, long time ago.

My Dearest Daughter,

Con, Happy Birthday! You are my brightest star, Lan. You make me the happiest father in the world.

You are my greatest treasure, my star, and my compass.

As you turn ten today, you must remember: Always be kind, always be clever, and always love.

My daughter, you are everything to me. Please don't grow up too quickly.

Tears stream down my face. My mind returns to when Ba gave me this very book, when he had wrapped it in orchid-patterned paper and set it on the dining table with a birthday cake and plenty of egg tarts. I hold the letter close to my chest, feeling its weight—feeling the love inked from Ba. No matter how long he's gone, I'll always remember.

I flip open the leather-bound notebook, and on a new page, I start writing. In the flickering candlelight, my hand glides across the page as words and words spill out of me. A sense of euphoria grips me, and I feel like I've broken through something. Like I can write again, and here I am, writing about a beautiful city that calls my name and the girl that exists with me within it.

The girl who shows me I am enough. That no matter what, I can write.

Chapter Twenty

VIVI

"You've been staring at that Google results page for an awfully long time. The consensus is that yes, Lan likes you. No need to ask an artificially intelligent thing."

Multiple Google tabs stare back at me: How to Tell if Someone Likes You and What Does It Mean When Your Crush Puts a Band-Aid on You. The results are mixed, with one camp advocating for *yes, they're totally into you* and another camp calling me absolutely delusional for even thinking so.

"This WikiHow has an outline of how to make your crush like you."

Cindy rolls her eyes. "You do not need all that. She. Likes. You."

"You are *one* opinion! And you're obviously biased toward me."

"Okay? The entire justice system is biased! Anyway, this jury of one has decided: Lan definitely has the hots for you."

My phone rings, saving me from more of Cindy's antics. My heart skips—maybe it's Lan—but then I see the caller ID from the FaceTime.

"It's my dad."

She gulps. "I'll . . . leave you alone to take the call."

Like a typical Vietnamese dad, mine only does two things with his phone: He posts a lot on Facebook and he sends a thumbs-up emoji to every one of my texts. He never calls. Unless something is wrong.

"Hi, Dad—"

Without even saying hi, he looks at me directly through the screen, and I can tell he's seeing through all my lies. "Con, you have to help me find Mom's photos. She's been freaking out."

I gulp, imagining Mom tearing our house apart searching for the photographs. The day I opened Mom's drawer and found them wedged between her immigration documents and visas, it was like something clicked. With those photos in my hands, Việt Nam didn't feel so far away anymore. They turned it into the place where our history began, where *Mom* was. "Why don't you tell her to forget about them for now? I'll help Mommy find them once I'm home."

Dad sighs. "I can't. Mom loves those photos. They . . . mean a lot to her."

The guilt that's been haunting me all semester returns. I didn't know these photos mean *that* much to her—after all, they seemed like something she didn't want to look at. I've never even once seen her take them out.

"What do the photos look like? I'll try to remember if I've seen them somewhere in the house." An outright lie. I'm ashamed of myself.

Dad inhales deeply, like he's not sure if he should be telling me or not. "They're photos she took with her from Việt Nam. Photos of her family."

"Very helpful, Dad." I try to lighten the mood. "I didn't know she had family in Việt Nam. She never said anything about them."

I hate that I can lie so easily.

"Well, con, she does. I think your grandma and aunt are still there, or that's what I've heard."

I want to scream, *I KNOW, DAD! I'M SO CLOSE TO FINDING THEM!* But instead I say, "Mom . . . hasn't told you anything about them?"

"When I met your mom, she . . . didn't want to talk about Việt Nam—at all. It was hard for me to understand how she felt, because I didn't remember anything—I hadn't been since I was such a little boy. I wanted to ask her all these questions about Sài Gòn and what it was like when she was growing up."

His words hurt, and it occurs to me then that, like me, Dad has been grappling with these feelings all his life. Like me, he's been feeling that push and pull between the United States and Việt Nam, not knowing where he fits in.

"What about Grandpa?" Surely he must have told Dad *something*. Grandpa lived there for most of his life.

Dad laughs a little. "No, no, your grandpa talked a lot, but he never wanted to mention anything related to Việt Nam. I think . . . it was really hard for him."

"How so?" I never got to meet my grandpa, but we had a portrait of him hanging in our hallway. It's strange, knowing of someone's face but never fully know them. All my memories of grandpa were just that, a framed photo existing in my childhood home.

"Tại vì," Dad continues. "Your grandpa had a lot of war trauma. But like all older Vietnamese folks, they just bottle it in."

This is the first time I've ever heard Dad talk about the war in Việt Nam. I had always assumed that Dad didn't have much to say, and it never occurred to me that, just like me, he wanted to know about Sài Gòn, but grew up with a parent who kept silent.

"What do you mean by war trauma?"

Dad sighs. "Your ông nội lived a long life in such a short time. Although he didn't say much, I'll always remember what he had told me. He was born in Hà Nội, but he didn't remember it because his family fled to Sài Gòn after the war started, when he was very young. He eventually joined the Southern Vietnamese government and after the war ended, we left. If we hadn't . . . I think Ông Nội would have been sent to a reeducation camp, and who knows what would have happened to me."

I didn't know that. Didn't know a lot of things. But ironically, being in Việt Nam has allowed me to know more and more—peeling back each layer in my family's history. Dad, like me, has been piecing together bits and fragments of everything.

"Do you remember leaving?"

Dad shakes his head. "No. I was too small. But your grandpa? He talked about it all the time. I think the journey gave him some claustrophobia. For the rest of his life, he'd disapprove of anything too small, too cramped, or too dirty."

"That . . . kind of sounds like Mom."

"Well, con, Mom was a boat person, too."

I blink. I'm not sure I want to understand what that means. "Boat person?"

Dad nods. "You know that a lot of people left Việt Nam after the war. The ones that left by sea—we call them boat people. Your mom was part of the last wave heading to the United States."

My mind whirls, and I realize I'd never thought about how Mom actually got to California. In my mind, she'd magically left Sài Gòn somehow and just never looked back. Growing up in Little Saigon, I knew of friends' family members who had immigrated from Việt Nam. I just never put it together that there's an encompassing term, *boat people*, and suddenly everything makes much more sense.

"How do you know all of this? Did Mom tell you?"

He chuckles softly. "No. When we met, Mom told me when she arrived in California, and the rest I sort of put together. You tend to learn a lot when you start talking to the older Vietnamese folks in

Little Saigon, especially if you're a stranger to them. I think, some-times, it's easier for people to say the things they've repressed for so long to someone they don't know. But with family? There's always that fear of being judged, of not knowing whether your family will still love you."

"I could never hate Mom."

"I know, con," Dad sighs. "But I understand if you're angry that you didn't know. When you're young, you can't help but resent them for not telling you. I know I did with Ông Nội."

"But you still love Ông Nội."

"Of course. It's a very, very hard thing that he did, becoming a ref-ugee. And though he didn't talk much about Việt Nam and our relation-ship wasn't the best, I'm still thankful that he loved me so much that he risked everything to give me a chance at survival. But love is so compli-cated, con. I knew he loved me, and I knew how important it was to be grateful—that he did everything for me. Still, I wanted to know about my mom and our country so badly."

I hadn't ever thought about Dad's relationship with Ông Nội and how he, too, has always felt all these complicated feelings about wanting to be grateful but also wanting to know so much more that guilt eats you alive. "How do you do it? How do you understand when the people you want answers from refuse to talk?"

Dad shakes his head. "I didn't. Con oi, sometimes, certain scars run too deep . . . and trying too hard to understand will just hurt the person you love."

"So I can never know? I should just . . . not pry and be a good daughter?"

Dad is silent, and I know it's because he understands what I'm trying to say. That for all my life, all I've ever wanted was for Mom to tell me about Việt Nam.

"I don't know, con. I didn't try, but . . . maybe you can."

I let his words and their implications linger between us over the phone. "Do you think she'll ever be ready?"

"Just remember, con, that at the end of the day, Mom and a lot of people just wanted hope. And that meant they had to leave home behind."

Chapter Twenty-One

LAN

Plates of ốc, gà chiên nướng mắm, water spinach with garlic, and a huge pot of lẩu thái spread across the dinner table. Grabbing the mortar and pestle, I grind more chilies into crushed red pepper paste for the fish sauce. Most important rule in every Vietnamese meal: Always have fish sauce nearby. Má, out in the garden, is tying silk lanterns onto our mango tree, her face glowing in their light. It's the Tết Trung Thu in Việt Nam, and my heart aches for Ba.

"You look happy," Má comments. "Did something good happen?"

"Oh, um." I hesitate. "I made a friend recently, and we've been trying a lot of street food together. We went to Chợ Bến Thành and are going to Bác Tuấn's cơm tấm restaurant."

"Good," Má says, relief in her eyes. "I'm glad you made a friend. You should be hanging out with people your age. Not with an old lady like me."

I wipe my hands before picking at the sleeves of my áo dài—it's a tradition both Má and I do every Trung Thu, wear our favorite áo dàis, have a meal and mooncakes together, and maybe light a lantern or two in our backyard.

"You're not old, Má. But you shouldn't be working so hard, either."

She waves her hand at me. "I should be the one to take care of us, and you should be out having fun, living your life."

I put down the mortar and pestle, unsure of what to make of Má's comments. I've always been taught that children should protect and take care of their parents, that we have an obligation to be there for the people who raised and fed us. Sure, some may say these are ridiculous Vietnamese filial piety expectations, but I believe in it—or at least I've convinced myself to—because in my case, Má only has me.

If not me, then who?

"I just don't want you to waste your youth, Lan," Má says.

I want to tell her that she shouldn't be wasting her youth, either, but deep down, I feel . . . happy to be going on street food dates with Vivi. Even just seeing her smile changes the monotonous pattern of what my days used to be like.

My phone lights up and I peek at the text, a blush forming across my cheeks immediately.

Vivi: Are you free? Cindy and I are thinking of going somewhere for Trung Thu.

"Did your friend text you?" Má asks, already plating the water spinach into her own bowl.

The usual excuses are clogged in my throat. I want to believe that it's okay to choose something for myself without feeling guilty.

"She's asking if . . . I can join her for Trung Thu."

"Go," Má says. "You should be out with a lantern in Chinatown watching the lion dancing! I'll be fine by myself—I already have the medicine here next to me, okay?"

I nod and get up, and she ushers me out the door. I fumble with my áo dài as I situate myself on the motorbike. Má hands me my helmet, fastening the clip for me.

"Cảm ơn, Má. I'll bring back mooncakes for you."

She smiles. "My favorite flavor?"

"Of course. Mooncakes with lots of lotus seeds inside."

Má waves me off as I drive away toward the bright skyline. The morning shops are already closed, making space for street food at night. Lively crowds flood through the streets of Sài Gòn, a warm glow emitting from almost everyone's hands—lanterns. Beautiful, luminous lanterns for the Mid-Autumn Festival.

Brushing my sweaty palms on my pink áo dài, I stare at the door to Vivi's dormitory. My heart rate increases with each passing second. Finally, the door opens and reveals a smiling face: Cindy. But no Vivi in sight.

"Sorry, Lan! We had some last-minute fashion issues. Vivi will be down soon."

Seconds later, a timid voice calls out from behind the door. "Cindy? Are you sure this is okay?"

Groaning, Cindy opens the door wide and pushes Vivi through. Vivi stumbles out with a yelp, nearly tripping on the pavement. I hurry to her side, my arms finding her waist as I break her fall.

"Hi," I manage to breathe out. Vivi's wearing the pale lavender áo dài from Cô Ngân, her inky-black hair brushed neat with a purple ribbon on top. "Purple looks good on you."

"Really?" she whispers, her cheeks rosy.

Cindy coughs and we break apart, both blushing. "Sorry we're late. This one"—she points at Vivi. "She took a bit deciding if she wanted to wear the áo dài or not. But I'm glad I managed to push her because you guys are matching!"

Vivi groans. "Thanks for predicting the future, Cindy."

"You're welcome." Cindy grins. "I'm going to join the rest of the study abroad cohort, *so*, why don't you two go ahead?"

Vivi gapes at Cindy, her face flustered—I wonder if she's shy at the thought of us spending time alone, even if we've been doing that so much already. "That's not what you said—" she starts.

"Bring her back by midnight, Lan!" Cindy says, scampering back into the dormitory before Vivi can catch her.

"So." I nudge us toward my motorbike, my heart thundering at the thought of us alone together again. Exploring Sài Gòn together again. "Ready for your first Trung Thu in this city?"

She nods, her arms finding their place over my hips. "Mooore than ready."

Because it's Trung Thu, Sài Gòn's traffic is a lot worse than most days. It takes us nearly an hour to get through the crowds, but we manage to make it to Chinatown just in time before the festival starts. Everywhere around us, children and adults are swarming toward stalls filled with mooncakes and tea. Brightly colored lanterns light up the alleyways from above. Amid the chatter, drumbeats cut through the air and vibrate through the alleyways, announcing that the lion dancing's about to start.

Vivi squeezes my hand as she points at the decorations above. "It's beautiful."

"Isn't it? Wait until you see the lion dancing. It's my favorite part."

"We also have lion dancing in Little Saigon! But it's so much more extravagant here. I feel like we're stepping through a different world. It's . . . magical."

We walk through Chinatown's alleyways, buying a box of mooncakes and sitting by the Sài Gòn River. Kids are running around us, all carrying at least one lantern in some shape or color.

"What are the kids doing?" Vivi asks.

"They're probably getting ready for the parade. Trung Thu is also known as the Children's Festival here, so parents would make lanterns for their kids—or just buy them—and the kids get to do a parade together, as a way of shining the way back to Earth for Cuội, the man who floated to the moon with his tree."

Sure enough, more children join in, carrying even more lanterns. They're forming a parade now, touring the alleyways while chanting rhymes alongside their parents.

"I want to join them," Vivi announces, and tugs me toward their direction, her eyes saying *Are you in?*

I pick up my pace, leading us to the crowd forming at Main Street. "Let's do it."

We weasel our way through the crowd, never letting go of each other's hands. People gravitate toward us, forming a circle as the drums and cymbals thunder through the air. A man in a round mask dressed in a red robe emerges, signaling the arrival of the lions. Ông Địa, or the Earth God, is at the heart of Trung Thu. The children gather around Ông Địa as he sways back and forth, light on his feet and clapping along to the drums. Two red lions—dancers in very elaborate sequined costumes—leap out from behind him, drawing squeals from everyone. Little kids hide behind the crowd, anxious about the beasts, some crying while their parents shush them with mooncakes. Vivi squeezes my hand, her eyes twinkling brightly like the lanterns above us. Their golden glow caresses her cheeks, and in this moment, she looks just like the fairy on the moon.

The lions make their way toward us, swaying their hips and heads along with the singing and cymbals. Ông Địa animatedly fans himself while the lions nuzzle up to Vivi and beg her to pet them. Cooing, she ruffles their manes and tosses coins into the straw hat carried by Ông Địa. Two more lions join us in the crowd, bouncing up and down as the crowd cheers them on. I take hundreds of pictures—of Vivi, of the two of us, of the colorful lanterns. I hope they'll remind her of Sài Gòn—of me.

Shifting closer to her, I shout in her ear. "Are you enjoying the festival?"

She nods, wrapping her arms around my shoulders and shouting back. "Let's go over there." She inclines her head toward a narrow alleyway with no vendors or shops, only dim light from the sunset and lanterns glowing through the vacant space.

I follow her. Following that warmth, that smile, and that girl who glows brighter than all the lanterns in the streets.

We're alone now, just us in this alleyway. Our fingers are still intertwined with one another. She looks at me quizzically. I feel the heat on my face. The tightness in my throat. The drums in my chest.

The wind blows gently past us, and her baby strands dance around her face. I smooth them behind her ears again, letting my hand caress her cheeks softly, slowly. The air around us is dizzying, electrifying, and I find myself leaning in, my eyes tracing the outlines of her face. I realize right then and there that I want this, whatever *this* is, and I want her. My mouth parts lightly on impulse, and my eyes search for hers—for the confirmation that she wants this as much as I do.

A heartbeat passes between us.

Then two.

"Vivi—"

"Yes," she answers, her eyelids fluttering as she closes the space between us. Her lips graze mine and fireworks explode in my brain. She arches her neck and I deepen the kiss, allowing her fingers to trail from my neck to my hair, and she tugs at my braid softly—heat rising from all the places that feel *good*.

My lips linger on hers, my breathing ragged as the urge to kiss her again and again overwhelms me. But before I can, Vivi speaks again. "I like you, Lan."

I cradle her cheeks between my palms, thumb brushing over the dimples I've been dreaming about. "Say it again."

She blushes profusely but doesn't let go, only staring at me, anticipating. "I like you."

"Again."

"I like you *so* much," she whispers.

I pull her toward my body, tilting her chin up. "How much is so much?"

"Like, a lot of bánh mì. A lifetime supply of bánh mì."

Laughing, I tug her close and our lips collide together again. We pour ourselves into each other as the sunset bleeds into Sài Gòn's skyline, two hearts beating louder than the bustling crowd of this city. Motorbikes are still blaring down the street, the sound of passersby echoing through the walls.

We stand there, heads on each other's shoulders, savoring the warmth radiating off our bodies. She nods shyly toward the entrance of the alleyway. "Someone will catch us."

I poke her nose lightly with mine and she laughs in my ear, a deep sound that rumbles through my core. "No one will care. Did you forget that it's Sài Gòn?"

She pulls herself from my arms, flushed from head to toe. "For the record, I didn't plan for this to happen."

"You didn't even daydream?"

"Maybe just a little bit," she squeaks.

I pull her back into my arms and plant kisses all over her face. One for each moment that she's made me happy, which is basically every moment that I'm with her. She leans into the kisses, returning the favor with her soft lips on mine. The smell of the Sài Gòn River clings to our clothes as we stay there in the alleyway, the glowing Trung Thu lanterns winking from above.

My Sài Gòn, I realize, is vibrant, full of life and, for me, full of love.

Chapter Twenty-Two

VIVI

All the movies and books prepare you for *that kiss* with the right person. That sparks will fly, and everything will feel *right*, they say. And God, how it felt so right with Lan. So much so that I didn't expect the post-kiss effects: the restlessness that grips me because I can't spend twenty-four seven with her, the way my mind only thinks of *her*, and how godawfully long it feels to wait for her when all I want to do is kiss her again and again and again.

A voice interrupts my thoughts. Finally. "Hey! Sorry, am I late?"

It's like my blood starts pumping faster the moment I look at Lan, and suddenly, everything is right in the world. "No. I wasn't waiting for long." I stood there waiting for fifteen minutes, because I couldn't wait to see her again.

She smiles, her hand grabbing mine naturally. "Ready for water puppetry?"

"A bit disappointed that it's not street food related, but anywhere with you? I'll be there."

Inside the Golden Dragon Water Puppet Theater is an amphitheater decorated with golden dragons and red, silky brocades. Paper lanterns crowd the ceilings, illuminating our path toward the open pool in front of us. A pagoda looms behind the pool, its arch the shape of two dragons' heads leaning together. Curtains with detailed embroidery of two dragons on each side and a sun in the middle create a backdrop for the stage. Around us, people float through the amphitheater, talking in a mix of Vietnamese and other languages.

I marvel at the sight, eyes glued to the towering space.

Lan chuckles, her laugh vibrating through my skin as she squeezes my hand. "Are you excited?"

"Why wouldn't I be? *But* I'm more excited to know the physics behind water puppetry. How long are they holding their breath for?"

Lan winks. "That's a secret. It's what makes this magical."

According to the pamphlet, the play for tonight is the fairy tale of the Dragon King and the Fairy Princess. The lights dim behind us, and we can hear the sound of water splashing. At once, the rhythmic sounds of cymbals, gongs, bamboo flutes, and monochords rip through the hall as fire flares from behind the curtains, announcing the start of the performance. Lan cracks a smile and plants a kiss on my cheek.

A voice booms from behind the curtains, making me jump in my seat. Beside me, Lan stifles a laugh.

"Welcome to the Golden Dragon Puppet Theater. Tonight's story is about the start of our country, and the birth of our people," the voice announces.

Puppets float from behind the silk curtains to the front of the pool in a single-file line, smoke swirling around them while the cymbals and gongs only speed up their rhythms. I notice the tallest water puppet, which is dressed in silky pink robes with a golden halo.

"That one reminds me of you," I whisper to Lan. "Look, it's wearing a braid just like you!"

"The short one in orange looks like you." She laughs in my ear, sending shivers up my spine again. "It's so little."

"That's *so* rude. But since it's from you, I'll take it."

As the applause dies down, the narrator starts the story.

This tale follows the story of Âu Cơ and Lạc Long Quân, the Fairy Princess and the Dragon King.

Âu Cơ, a kind and beautiful fairy, was traveling one day when a crane appeared in front of her by the roadside, bleeding and injured.

"Help me," it cried.

Âu Cơ, overwhelmed with hurt for the poor creature, nursed it under her care. "Friend, please stay strong," she whispered. Together, Âu Cơ and the crane spent five days and five nights together under the sun, the moon, and the stars. They watched flowers grow and rain fall from the sky. They danced through the rice fields. Once the crane was all better, it bade farewell to Âu Cơ.

"Goodbye, my friend." The crane thanked Âu Cơ. "Thank you for your kindness. Heaven blesses you."

A few days later, as Âu Cơ continued her journey, she encountered a giant water beast. Frightened, she tried turning into a bird to fly away, but the beast caught her before she could.

"Please, let me go!"

Her cries reached the heavens, and the crane she'd saved appeared just in time. This time, it wasn't just a crane—it was the mighty Dragon God. The Dragon called upon the sea and, with his magic, saved Âu Cơ.

"My friend, you came for me! Thank you." Âu Cơ was happy to see her friend, and once she was healed, the two reunited with a long embrace. But to Âu Cơ's surprise, the body of the Dragon God melted and revealed a handsome young man.

"Âu Cơ, I am Lạc Long Quân, God of Dragons and the Sea, and I wish for your hand in marriage.

So with the blessing of the Dragon Goddess of the Sea and Sky and the

Fairy King, Âu Cơ and Lạc Long Quân's love created the beautiful country of Việt Nam. Together, they bore one hundred eggs from which hatched one hundred humans—the first humans of the kingdom of Lạc Việt.

"*Eggs?*" I whisper to Lan, earning side eyes from the people around us. "Like, chicken eggs?"

She quirks an eyebrow. "What do you have against eggs?"

"Nothing. Love them in my food. Just can't imagine humans coming out of them."

She laughs, and someone nearby shushes us. "It's a *fairy tale.*"

"So, you're saying it's a happy ending?"

It's Lan's turn to shush me. "I'm not saying anything. Just watch."

After a hundred years of living together on land with Âu Cơ, the Dragon King yearned for the sea. And so, he told his wife that he must leave.

"*Âu Cơ, my dear, I must return to the sea. You are the land, and I am the sea. And though I've only lived in happiness with you, I cannot bear to be away from my home any longer.*"

Âu Cơ sobbed, begging her husband to stay with her. Alas, it was their children who convinced her.

"*We love both of you. But Father is right, we must come back to the sea and build our empire. That is our home, too,*" *their eldest said.*

Respecting Lạc Long Quân's wishes, Âu Cơ agreed. "*Please send me signs that you still love me.*"

The Dragon King nodded. "*Every day, when the sun kisses the ocean, its rays will turn into a brilliant red just for you. I will protect you and our children. I will make sure that your mountains, your trees, and your flowers are always dancing to my rain. That your rivers, your streams, and your lakes are always full. That together, we will raise a kingdom mankind can only dream of.*"

Fifty children followed their father to the sea while fifty followed their mother to the mountains. But although they parted ways, one promise remained: If they were to encounter one another, they must treat one another like family.

With their father, the fifty children learned how to fish, hunt, and fight. Âu Cơ, on the other hand, taught her children the art of harvest, how to breed animals, and how to build houses. It is said that the art of cooking from bamboo tubes was taught to our ancestors by Âu Cơ herself.

From Lạc Long Quân and Âu Cơ's descendants came the ancestors of Lạc Việt, and today, the ancestors of Việt Nam. It is said that the Vietnamese people inherited Lạc Long Quân's strength and perseverance but also Âu Cơ's kindness and intelligence. In the end, Lạc Long Quân and Âu Cơ's children taught us that regardless of where we come from, we all must help one another—for we are all Vietnamese.

The end.

Still sniffling, I wipe my tears with my sleeve. "That was so sad! They had to leave each other!"

Lan laughs beside me, our hands still intertwined—they have been this entire time. "It's not that bad. They still love each other. They just had to do what was necessary for them."

"How do you leave the people you love?"

She looks away, pointing her gaze at the center of the stage, where the puppets are retreating behind the curtains. "I'm not sure. But I think, sometimes, you have to do what's right for you—even if you may lose the people you love most."

Sometimes, when Lan speaks of these things, I can't help but wonder if she ever thinks about leaving Sài Gòn. It makes me think of Mom, too, if somewhere deep in Mom's heart she still thinks about the family she has here. If it kills Mom to not see them again.

I clear my throat. "Thanks for coming along with me . . . but I should get back to the dormitory soon. I have class in the morning."

There's a delicate balance to tread after you confess to someone that you like them, and you find out that they also like you back. All I want is to spend every waking second with Lan, to even just sit like this in an amphitheater by ourselves and talk about anything. But I don't know where we are—what we are—and suddenly, I'm all too aware of how she reacts to everything I say. If I'm being annoying. If I'm too much. If I say the wrong things and want more than what we are and . . . she pushes me away.

To my surprise, her grip on my hand tightens, and warmth floods through my body as she maneuvers us out of the theater and weaves through the crowd of people returning home. My skin sings against hers, and my stomach somersaults with each step we take. It's like we're a scene out of a movie, running to who knows where—but with her, I'd go anywhere.

"You can't go to sleep yet! This is the best time to get on a xích lô ride."

"Xích lô . . . ride?" The same embarrassment all semester returns— the feeling that I don't know enough about Vietnamese culture, that no matter what, I can't ever be . . . Vietnamese. Still, Lan doesn't judge. Instead, she seems *excited*.

"The best and only touristy thing you should be doing," she says. "They're these cyclo-ride businesses that take you through the city." She tugs me toward a party of cyclos, the uncles perching on top while waiting for customers. The xích lô resemble tricycles but with a wide bench seat in the back.

We get on a xích lô together, squished into the cramped and leath- ery driver-powered machine. I lean back against the seat, acutely aware of how our arms are touching. How, if I want to, I can kiss her right now.

But then she turns to me, smiling, and all I want to do is stare at how perfectly shaped her lips are and how her cheeks are flushed because of the humidity. "Are you ready?" she asks.

I nod, my gaze still focused on her. "Yeah."

Our xích lô snakes through the current of motorbikes, merging into the crowd as motorcycle fumes cling to our hair. The motion is abrupt, and unlike car rides, I can feel every pothole and bump on the road. We loop through historic Sài Gòn, the lights of the city illuminating our faces. I watch Lan's eyes marvel at the skyline, and I wonder how long it's been since she's looked at the city with so much *awe*. If she ever did at all.

Another xích lô ride comes up next to us, and the two passengers grin and wave at us. They're wearing matching T-shirts that say HER WIFE with arrows pointing at each other. They look so goofy that I have to laugh. Lan turns her head, meeting my eyes, and bursts out laughing as well.

"How do you like it?" she asks, her eyes studying my mouth. I swallow, not sure how to answer her because my eyes haven't left her face. At all. Even now, I'm only focusing on the upturned corners of her mouth.

A breath hitches in my throat as I watch her face in front of me, tracing every line, every detail. "Beautiful," I breathe out.

I lean in, allowing the pull of my heart to guide me. Fluttering my eyes closed, I brush my fingers past her cheeks, through her hair, and down her neck. Shivering beneath my touch, she presses me closer. Her arms on my waist are a searing heat while electricity runs through my body and explodes like butterflies in my stomach.

Chapter Twenty-Three

LAN

The sticky air clings to my back and I tug at my shirt in hopes of making the sweat disappear as I water the orchids. The air smells of wet soil, while the leaves from our mango tree litter the ground. My fingers reach toward a flower, caressing a blushing pink petal, and I watch the droplets roll off its stem. The orchid stares back at me, and in a fleeting moment, I can see Vivi's face within the blossom.

"Lan? Ready to go?"

I aim the hose directly at Triết's face. "Don't scare me like that."

He pours himself coffee, then gulps it down before fastening the belt to our bánh mì cart. "Stop daydreaming about *someone* and come help me open. You're wasting time."

I roll my eyes, still aiming the hose at him threateningly. "I cannot believe you're the one telling me that." Normally, I'd be hustling Triết out the door.

The shutter opens and Má steps out, carrying a basket. "Why are you both bickering so early in the morning again? Stop looking so angry; you'll wrinkle your faces later in life."

Triết pulls out a small mirror from his pocket, dutifully checking every pore on his face and every hair on his head. "No way. Lan, this is your fault for making me age."

"Or maybe you should wear more sunscreen," I retort.

"I don't need sunscreen. The Vietnamese genes absorb all UV rays and make us glow."

"Oh, stop it." Má swats at both of us, a smile on her face. "Triết has something important to say."

My heart drops. I've readied myself for the inevitable day when Triết would leave, and the house with the mango tree would be home to just two people again. Still, I want to hold on to these days in Sài Gòn with him and Má as much as possible. Bottle these moments up and hold them tight, because I'm scared. So scared of the person Má might become once he leaves, and scared of who I will be.

But he's not bound to us, and familial obligations or not, I've accepted that Má will be the only constant for me, just as I'll always be by her side, the only daughter through it all.

"I got a job," Triết says, and at once, the world stops spinning beneath my feet.

"What?" I ask, not believing my ears. "Are you leaving? Are you not working at the bánh mì stall anymore? Are you not living with us—"

Triết plops a hat on my head, breaking my spiral as he adjusts the cap for me, and the instant coolness shields my face. "The internship is with a Vietnamese airline based in Sài Gòn, so I'll need to figure out my schedule with them, but other than that, I'm not going anywhere. I know you're telling yourself I'll be leaving soon, and you'll be all alone. But you won't be."

"I don't think that," I say begrudgingly. Am I that easy to read?

"You so do. You're already making a checklist of things to do once I leave. You plan for catastrophes so it's easier to run."

"So, you're saying don't plan?"

"I'm just saying to *trust me*."

Má comes up behind me, and my stomach flips when I realize I had almost forgotten her presence, too caught up in my back-and-forth with Triết. Má heard all my questions about where Triết would be and what that would mean for us. She heard that I, her daughter, plan for the worst because I'm scared. I don't want Má to think I'm scared. I want her to know that whatever happens, she can trust me. She can always lean on me.

"Con à." Má turns to me. "Triết isn't going anywhere. He's our family."

I wonder if Má is saying that for both of us, and that if we say it enough, we'll start to believe it, too. For all my plans and checklists, I don't want to imagine a day without Triết—just as I'm refusing to think about the day Vivi will leave, back to her life in California, and I'll be left in this city that's too big for a lonely girl.

Má's hand finds my back, her left one reaching for my face. "Con, you don't need to worry about our family. Let Má do the worrying. Let Má take care of you."

The words fall over me like a warm hug, and for once, I do more than nod at what she said—I reach for her, my arms finding her strong back.

"Why don't we all take the day off?" Má pulls apart from me, but her hand is still on my shoulder. "It's ngày giỗ for your dad."

Ba's death anniversary, the day he left us four years ago. "I totally . . . forgot."

Má's gaze softens. "Dates are arbitrary. What's important is how we remember him, how we honor him after his death. And you already do so much of that, con."

There are so many things still unsaid between us, but for now, I hold on to her words and their comfort. "How should we celebrate his day?"

She smiles, wide. "Help me with the altar, will you?"

In Vietnamese culture, death is celebrated. It's the crossing to the afterlife, where Ba is meant to rest peacefully, and so families often gather during ngày giỗ to cook big meals and remember the people that are watching over us. The first anniversary was hard, because how were Má and I supposed to celebrate Ba's death? We wanted him back. But this year, the fourth year, I'm finding it easier to accept. To remember him somehow, to let his memories within us live on.

We've always had Ba's altar in our home, his portrait watching over us in the living room. But today, it feels right to cúng—or to invite him home—with the mango trees and the orchids he loved.

Under the towering mango tree, we set up an altar for Ba's portrait. Leaves rustle from above as birds wake, and the lanterns from Trung Thu, still tied to the branches, sway softly. Ba loved the lanterns, and I remember we'd hang them on this same mango tree together. How odd, that a tree survived Ba. I wonder if it'll live on after me, too, and if this same tree will remember me and everyone in our small home.

Má carefully arranges the offerings under the tree. Ba's portrait sits in the center, embraced by the fruits from our garden: bananas, mangos, dragon fruits, lychees. Beside them is a steaming bowl of thịt kho with bamboo shoots and quail eggs. I place a pot of white orchids by the altar, and it feels right to have Ba's flowers next to him. I wonder if he's watching us. If he's proud of me. We unfurl the incense holder from its bag before grabbing a stick and lighting the tip. Shaping my lips into an O, I gently blow on the incense. Smoke rises from the stick, and I wonder if this was what Ba meant when he told me—a long, long time ago—that incenses were smoldering, hazy maps for souls to find their way through the world. The smoke curls around our bodies as I crinkle my temple and bow three times, each time with a story rather than a prayer.

Ba, we have been good. We miss you more than anything, but we're learning to live without you.

Ba, I'm writing again. I've found strength in me to pick up my pen, but I'll never forget you're the one that started my love for it.

Ba, I've met someone, and I hope I never lose her.

With a long exhale, we blow on the smoke, careful to not extinguish the flame. I stick the incense back in the holder and bow one last time. Má takes my hand as I grab Triết's, and the three of us pay our respects to Ba. This is one of those moments that I want to wrap tightly in my memory and never let go.

My phone chimes. Then it chimes again. Only one person texts me like that, and the thought of her makes me blush.

"Go," Má whispers. "It's your friend, isn't it?"

Nodding, I mouth her a "Thank you" and call Vivi. I close the gate to our home, my legs carrying me through the alleyways in my neighborhood as I sidestep puddles and potholes. "Hello?"

Vivi sighs on the other end of the line, and my heart leaps. "Hey. I miss you."

All the warm and fuzzy feelings return, and I will myself not to run straight to Vivi's dorm right then and there. "I miss you, too. Did you need something?"

I wince, knowing how odd that sounds. Not that Vivi needs a reason to call me, but ever since I realized I like her, words haven't felt right on my tongue. Instead, they're jumbled, and sometimes I don't know how to express all the dizzying things she makes me feel. Still, my heart thrums with anticipation for her answer.

Her giggles ring through my ear. "I wanted to talk to you more. Is that enough?"

My heart has got to stop pounding so loudly. "Yeah. It is. More than enough."

"What are you doing right now?"

I glance at my surroundings, but my thoughts zero in on the simple fact that Vivi called because she cares about me. She wants to know what I'm doing just as much as I've been thinking about her and her day and—

I clear my throat. "I'm walking through my neighborhood. My mom and Triết are tidying up my dad's altar right now. It's his death anniversary."

"Oh." She sucks in a breath. "Do you want me to leave you alone?"

"No, it's okay." This time, I actually believe myself. "For some reason this year, I haven't felt as sad today—when I'm reminded of my dad's passing—and I think it's because of you."

"Really? Why?"

"Because I have something to look forward to every day: seeing you, working on the contest application together. And . . . Sài Gòn has been less lonely with you in it."

I can feel her smiling through the phone. "I don't think I would've fallen in love with this city if I hadn't met you. I don't think I would've had the courage to come to Sài Gòn if I hadn't found you years ago on the internet. I think Sài Gòn would just be another place on the map for me, not a city where someone important to me lives."

My heart pounds, but I still can't shake off the anxiety that all this is temporary. That Vivi will inevitably leave. Unable to say anything, I drink in her words. That's the only thing I know how to do now, to let Vivi's words envelop me, and to fall right into their embrace.

"I don't think I deserve all those compliments."

She laughs, and I press the phone closer to my ear—imagining her right next to me. "You have no idea how much . . . you've done for me."

I take in my neighborhood stretching before me, noticing the lone corner market at the end of the street. It seems more vibrant, a brighter shade of pink. I picture Ba and me perching on the stools next to the flan lady, devouring sweet custard during hot summer days. I think about Chú Hai on his bicycle every Saturday, passing out extra loaves of bread for everyone.

"Because of you," I say, "I think I've finally learned how special this place I call home really is."

Chapter Twenty-Four

VIVI

I'm perched on a blue plastic stool just outside the dorm, listening to the noise of the city: motorbike horns blaring, people haggling at the shops, friends chattering as they walk by. I have a cà phê sữa and a pile of schoolbooks to my left on the plastic table and a plate of gỏi cuốn from Bà Hai on my lap. It's funny how quickly I've gotten used to living in Sài Gòn. These plastic stools will always remind me of my time here, and of Lan, because of all the street food dates we've gone on. The tall fan from the dormitory hums loudly through the window, trying its best to oscillate the heat away but alas, failing.

I'm distracted, and instead of doing my homework, I'm staring at the spread in front of me on the plastic table under the sun—all the photos of Mom in Việt Nam. There's the photo of Mom and her family in front of Chợ Bến Thành, another of Mom in jeans and a T-shirt with street food stalls in the background, and various images of Mom in different spots throughout Sài Gòn. Mom before a towering cathedral. Mom in front of kites. Mom outside of an amphitheater. Mom on a xích lô.

All this time, I've been retracing her life in Việt Nam, matching her footsteps to mine without even knowing. The closer I examine the photos, the more I see my own face looking right back at me. It's weird, thinking about Mom around my own age living in this city, just like I'm doing now. Our lives intertwining a generation later.

"Hey!" Lan hovers in front of our plastic table outside the dormitory, two sugarcane pouches in her hand. "Ready to go?" she says breathlessly, sweat on her neck. She looks radiant.

"Yeah." I lace my hand through hers. It's so natural now. This, *us*.

"You're looking at those photos again?"

"I keep hoping . . . that I can find something to lead us closer to where my family is from these pictures. What about this cathedral?"

Lan chews on her lips, and I know from the way her brows scrunch that she doesn't know, either. "I'm sorry, Vivi."

"But," she continues, "Bà Ngân said Bác Tuấn from the restaurant knows your family. Let's see what he has to say. If he doesn't know, then I promise you, Vivi, I'll do anything to find them for you."

My heart lurches at her declaration, and all the sadness wilts, replaced by a soaring kind of feeling that's more than *like*, and I know that Lan means more than just a crush. More than a girl I trade kisses with.

We drive under the towering hoa phượng trees, their bright red blossoms littering the sidewalk. We pass by a high school, students mingling at the gate. Some are wearing white áo dàis while others are in white button-ups and navy pants. My mind imagines a life where Lan and I are classmates, riding our bikes to school together, pressing hoa phượng petals into pages together.

Petals dance around us, and I extend my hand to grab a fluttering hoa phượng and tuck the blossom behind Lan's ear.

"What's this for?"

I peck her cheek, immediately seeing how flushed she is. "It's a thank-you."

We hop off the motorbike and walk by the bustling street food vendors just outside the high school's gates. Motorbikes are speeding through the street, some carrying tons of mangoes, flowers, and rice sacks on the back seats. We cross the street to a tall building divided into concrete grids, where each square has its own personality: warm fairy lights strung through the windows, blue and neon coffee signs, plants growing over the weather-stained gray slabs between units. Each square looks like a portal to another world.

"Come on!" Lan grabs my hand this time, my heart and legs racing to catch up with her.

Excitement buzzes through me as I gape at the building and at how Lan expertly guides us through the crowd, but as we approach the cơm tấm restaurant, the same anxiety from Chợ Bến Thành creeps up my spine.

What if this uncle doesn't know? What if this is our dead-end road?

Or, what if he does, and it turns out my family is in this city, and I can actually meet them? What then? How do I go from there? Where do Mom and I go from there? What will become of our relationship?

"Are you okay?" Lan snaps me from my thoughts, the same worried face she showed at Chợ Bến Thành. It strikes me how observant she is, and how well she knows me.

I inhale deeply, willing the anxiety to subside. "I'm as good as I can be. You said the cơm tấm here is the best, right?"

"The best you can get in Sài Gòn."

I nod. "At least good food will comfort me."

Cơm Tấm Thiên Thảo is tightly packed with guests, and more students our age trickle in, colorful backpacks with matching key chains on their shoulders as they trade laughs and food without a care in the world. There's something so intimate about a group of friends eating together that I can't take my eyes off them, and I find myself wishing for the same life: to live in a city where I have deep roots, to have street food so abundant I'll never run out of options, and to do everything that's Vietnamese. How would my life have turned out if Mom or Dad had never left this country? How would I have grown up?

Would I still have met Lan?

"So." Lan returns from the front counter, placing matching cơm tấm plates on our table. The broken rice is plated neatly next to sides of a pork chop, a sunny-side-up egg, a steamed omelet next to tomatoes, cucumbers, and garnished with pickled radish and carrots. "Bác Tuấn will be out soon. His daughter told us to eat first."

I stare at the plates, my mouth watering. "This place is family owned?"

She nods. "A lot of restaurants and street food businesses are family owned and family operated. They usually employ relatives' siblings, cousins, or kids."

"That's cool. It's like a tradition."

Lan visibly squirms at my comment. "I guess so."

Did I say something wrong? Is it not cool to have a family business, something so special to you and your family?

"How did Bánh Mì 98 start?"

"It's been passed down through my family for generations. It was my dad's world—that stall meant everything to him. He loved making food, but he loved meeting people even more. You should have seen it years ago, when there'd be a line stretching for almost two kilometers and everyone knew his name. Then my mom and I took over when he passed."

Lan's eyes sparkle as they always do when she talks about her dad. Usually, the sparkle would be followed by a sadness sweeping across her face—but not this time, as if the memory no longer hurts her as it did when we first met.

"Do you want to . . . do that for the rest of your life? Take care of the bánh mì stall?"

She squirms again. "I don't know. But like you said, it's family tradition—right?"

"That doesn't mean you have to run the bánh mì stall for the rest of your life. Family tradition or not, you should do what you want."

She inhales deeply, her voice almost shaking. "It's a lot more complicated than that. Bánh Mì 98 has been my grandparents' parents' business passed down to Ba. How could I ever just let it go? The bánh mì stall is bigger than just me, it's a Phan family treasure."

I want to tell Lan that there's nothing more important than her and her happiness, and that she should live her life how she wants—not tied down by any burdens or family expectations. But before I can, a man in his fifties makes a beeline toward our table, knocking over a guest and their chair in the process, before enveloping Lan in a tight hug.

"Bé Lan! How are you? I haven't seen you in so long!"

She hugs him back, a wide grin matching his. "Chào Bác Tuấn! Bác have to stop calling me bé. I'm not a kid anymore."

"Tch." He pretends to be offended. "You will always be our little girl. Have you been well? And your mom?"

I steal a glance at Lan, preparing to comfort her—or do anything—because I know how difficult that question is for her; how does she do it, smile for people when it's still so hard living with grief?

Lan, as expected, keeps her smile and bows again, thanking the uncle for his caring questions. "I've been good, Bác. Very good, actually. This is Vivi, and we've been exploring Sài Gòn together because she's a study abroad student. I wanted to show her your cơm tấm, she just can't leave without trying it at least once." Lan expertly sneaks in a compliment. Even I recognize that strategy: Pamper up the Vietnamese adults with compliments before asking them the real, important question.

"Vivi! Welcome to Việt Nam," Bác Tuấn says warmly. "I hope you're enjoying your stay here. Bé Lan knows everything about Sài Gòn."

I nod enthusiastically, excitement coursing through me. It's nice, being welcomed by other Vietnamese people. "Cảm ơn, Bác. Lan is really the best."

Her cheeks turn pink at my comment.

"Now, is the food that bad that you both haven't eaten any?"

Oh. Right. We were so caught up in our conversation that the cơm tấm turned room-temperature warm, and the ice in our water cups already melted.

"Xin lỗi, Bác," Lan apologizes, and I repeat after her, even including a bow.

"Con ah, I'm just teasing, but eat—you both look so skinny!"

I stifle back a laugh, but Bác Tuấn's comment reminds me of Mom. Growing up among Vietnamese people in Little Saigon, I've learned they express love and care through two questions: Have you eaten? And, why are you so skinny? Mom always says that to be happy, you must be full.

Taking a bite, I dip the grilled pork into the sweet and sour nước mắm and pair it with a spoonful of cucumbers and rice. The charred taste of the grilled pork combined with the sweetness of the nước mắm and the coolness of the cucumbers hum in unison inside my mouth. "Is this rice . . . really broken?"

Lan bursts out laughing at my, quite frankly, stupid question. But hey, cơm tấm means "broken rice," and no one has ever told me why.

"Yes, Vivi. The rice grains are really fragmented," she says.

"But do you both know why we only use broken rice grains?" Bác Tuấn asks, smiling at me now.

"Because it tastes good?" I try, unsure of what to say.

Bác Tuấn laughs. "That is true. But the story is, during times when things were so bad and people only had broken rice to eat and whole grain rice was a luxury, we created something filling out of poverty. Now the food is a popular Vietnamese cultural dish."

"Wow. That's a fascinating origin story." The plate I'm eating from feels oddly important. This very plate of cơm tấm embodies hope and survival—and it makes me think of Mom and her family, too. Whether or not they had enough food to eat, if they ate broken rice grains, and the continuous question of what their lives were like. It's strange, to be eating the dish they probably ate to survive years later as a tourist in my family's home country.

I can see Lan nodding next to me, her eyes bright as she keenly listens to Bác Tuấn. It's no wonder that Lan's so passionate about Vietnamese food and its stories when everyone in her life is the same.

"Not just this dish, either," Bác Tuấn continues. "Vietnamese food is so important to our history. Did you know that out of ten million people that live in Sài Gòn, about one million get their livelihood from selling street food?"

Lan and I both shake our heads. "I didn't. But that makes sense, street food is everywhere in this city," she says.

I nod. From what I've learned, street food is the soul of Sài Gòn.

"But enough about food—I could go on and on all day." Bác Tuấn turns to me. "Con, you look like you have an important question to ask me."

I'm almost caught off guard by his bluntness, almost, until I remember that's just how Vietnamese people are. Straight to the point. No beating around the bush. I hand him the photograph of Mom's family in front of Chợ Bến Thành, the question I've tossed and turned all night over slipping out of my mouth. "Do you . . . know who these people are?"

"Of course," he says right away. "I went to high school with Hoa and Hiền. We didn't know each other well, but I should have more photos of them."

My mind races with the information revealed to me: Hoa, Mom's name, and Hiền, my aunt's name. Flower and Gentleness. One step closer to my family's life in Việt Nam.

Bác Tuấn rummages through the back of the restaurant and returns with a photo album, smoothing out an old photograph of a group of students in front of a section of Sài Gòn unfamiliar to me.

"This was during our field trip to Bến Nghé, the Old French Quarter in District One."

My eyes zero in on the non-Vietnamese architecture in the background. "The buildings, did you say that they're French?"

Bác Tuấn nods. "That's the Opera House and the City Hall, both built in the style of French colonial architecture."

I remember what I had learned from *A Bánh Mì for Two* before coming to Sài Gòn: French imperialism in Vietnam.

As if reading my mind, Lan jumps in. "Even after independence, traces of imperialism remain. Not only the French, but also the Americans and the Japanese, too."

"Like phở and bánh mì," I say aloud. "From the architecture to food . . . the cultural influences are everywhere."

"Yes, but," Bác Tuấn says, "it's more than cultural influences. Vietnamese people are strong. We fought for freedom, and even if these influences linger, we've made them ours. We invented phở from pot-au-feu and bánh mì from baguettes. These buildings are now a part of Sài Gòn. There's so much history within this city."

"I know." I nod. "Being in this city makes me feel small but in a good way. Like my life is so tiny compared to the bigness of Sài Gòn and all of its history."

Lan's looking at me across the table, her gaze sending a tingling feeling throughout my body. "Because of Vivi, I'm learning how special this city is," she says, her eyes not leaving mine.

I clear my throat and turn to Bác Tuấn. "Are these the students from your high school in the photograph?"

Bác Tuấn nods and points to the two girls in the back smiling with perfect teeth, both pointing to something out of frame. "That's Hoa and

Hiền. They're only a year apart, but they were best friends. They also had the biggest opinions in class, Hoa especially—she was known as the feisty girl. Pick on Hiền? Hoa will beat you up."

I chew on my lip—is that really Mom? Mom who never really says much? What changed? How weird it is to be looking at my aunt through a photograph, a moment captured long before I was born, and to hear about her life from a stranger. I wonder if Aunt Hiền still talks to Mom, if she knows about me.

"How do you know Hoa and Hiền?" Bác Tuấn asks, and I swallow. I'm not ready to tell him, or anyone except Lan, about my mom and her story. "Someone I know is looking for Hiền," I say instead. "Do you . . . know where she might be now?"

Bác Tuấn looks at me, and I can see understanding passing through his face. Maybe he notices my cheekbones or my nose—whatever similar features I share with the women in the photo. "Last I heard, they live in District 2. Hoa and Hiền's mom used to sell bánh bao in Thủ Thiêm. If you ask around there, I'm sure someone will know."

If there's one thing I know for sure about Mom, it's that bánh bao is her comfort food. Bad day at work? She'll sit through Little Saigon traffic congestion for a dozen bánh bao from her favorite bakery. Me leaving for "Singapore"? She'll stuff my bag with bánh bao for the flight. Now the food that's always been a part of my life seems way more important than it had ever been. It means something to Mom, and I wonder if it's because she misses Sài Gòn.

"But," Lan starts, her voice seemingly unsure, and my chest lurches. "There are so many bánh bao stalls in Thủ Thiêm. We don't even know if that one stall is still there."

"It's not." Bác nods solemnly before massaging his temple in thought. "But I do remember a cathedral being by their home."

"The cathedral from the photograph." My heart beats faster. I could see it now, the route to Mom's childhood home—to my answers—just waiting for me in Distict 2.

"If you ask the people around the cathedral, they should know of Hoa and Hiền."

"Cảm ơn, Bác," I say, a heavy weight in my chest. Every time we make progress and I learn more, the less I know how to feel. I'll go to Thủ Đức City and find my family, and then . . . what?

"Hey." Lan nudges me and points to the left corner of the restaurant, where students are flocking to one another with pens and Post-it notes in their hands, scribbling something onto the sticky notes. "Why don't we go over there?"

We excuse ourselves from Bác Tuấn and thank him for everything. I keep bowing, and Bác keeps insisting the food is on the house. I finally take in the rest of the restaurant, my eyes observing every nook and cranny. Yellow wallpaper brightens the small space. An oval bamboo light fixture glows warmly from the ceiling. Paintings of Việt Nam hang on the walls, some of Hội An and others of Hà Nội—places I've always wanted to visit. Finally, one little corner is decorated with paper flowers, lanterns, and an explosion of colorful sticky notes.

A tiny chalkboard reads *Question of the Day: Where is your favorite place to eat?*

Other people posted their favorite restaurants and street food stalls, and as my eyes glide over each answer on the wall, something important stares back at me.

"Lan! Some of these answers thank *A Bánh Mì for Two* for helping them find their favorite places!" I say excitedly, keeping my voice hushed in case she doesn't want people to know.

At first, she doesn't say anything and just continues staring at the wall, awe on her face. "Tell me I'm not dreaming. That this is real. People actually wrote down *A Bánh Mì for Two*?"

"It's real," I say, and reach for a sticky note myself. "I would write the same thing, but I already know what I want to put on the wall."

"What are you writing down?"

I show her my sticky note: *My favorite place to eat is anywhere with you.*

She smiles. "That's funny, because I'm about to write the same thing."

Chapter Twenty-Five

LAN

Warm arms embrace me as a soft body crashes into my back. "Hi, Vivi."

"Hi." She nuzzles her face in my neck. With one hand, she tucks loose strands from my hair and dabs my sweat with her sleeve. "There. I've always wanted to do that."

"Wipe my sweat for me?"

She blushes. "Yeah."

When you like someone, I've realized, everything they do matters to you. Everything they do suddenly becomes intimate, and I find myself wishing to remember every word she says to me. Everything she does for me. All my thoughts point to Vivi.

She laces her fingers through mine, nudging us toward the street and away from the stall. "Come onnn, we have to submit the application by midnight."

"You sure the story is good enough?"

I used to look forward to finishing that Sài Gòn blog post with her. I imagined that I could hit submit and maybe—just maybe—I'd win, and everything would turn out better for Má and me. But today, the day we're submitting the application together, I want to drag my feet for as long as possible. Where will Vivi and I go from here? Will we still talk after the contest?

Her gaze softens, and she reaches to tuck a strand behind my ear. "We've done everything we can."

I nod, feeling heat creeping up my spine. I wipe away the bánh mì crumbs on my pants and match her pace, admiring how she bounces on her feet, taking each step without a care in the world.

We stop short in front of the tall building made of gray slabs and weather-stained walls. The door is left open as I predicted, and from below, I can see the plumeria tree at the very top.

Vivi scrunches her brows at the winding staircase. "You're kidding. We're climbing this?"

"Come on! It's not that bad."

The stairs still smell of mildew, and the cracked concrete greets me. Only, they aren't greeting just me this time. Our steps echo in sync with our breath, sandals squeaking as we race up the stairs. I can see beads of sweat on her neck as she runs ahead, and at once, I understand her earlier urge to dab my sweat away. People in Sài Gòn look microscopic from this high up, like I zoomed out of my own bubble and am watching everyone else's. People huddling together outside their homes, children and their parents slurping up hu ties, and shops closing for the day. The skyscraper's light replaces the sun as the boats on the river glow brightly. It's strange to think that seconds ago, I was down there, also existing within that world of this city.

Still, there's something special about watching this world from above, and I can hear it in Vivi's gasp. "You're right. This is *the* place to submit the application. I think just being up here will give us even more luck."

I nod. "Doesn't Sài Gòn look so different from up here?"

"It's symbolic, too. Looking down at the city you're writing about as we submit the story."

I lead her closer to the edge of the rooftop, taking off my shoes. She does the same, giggling at the rough sensation from the wet concrete. The sun sets in the distance, already dipping below the skyline. I notice how tan Vivi got over the past few months; freckles now sprinkle across her arms like stars.

I take out the laptop from my backpack, opening the page to the submission portal. "You already know . . . how much all this means to me—this contest, the fact that it could literally change my life. When I reread the story we wrote, I knew there was something missing. Don't get me wrong, everything seemed perfect. Except, I had to add in one more thing, one more person, or else I'd regret it. *You.*"

She furrows her brows. "Me?"

I nod. "You remind me to write about the people that I love. The people that inspire me. I wrote about how Sài Gòn seems brighter, more beautiful because of someone I had met recently. Someone that allows me to stop looking outside of Sài Gòn and yearning for what I don't have. Someone that reminds me to hold what's in front of me, to treasure the beauty of this city."

"I really did all that?" She faces me.

I laugh and press my cheek against hers. "That story was the best thing I've ever written. Because you helped me write it."

"But it was all you. You're the one that wrote the actual words."

I shake my head. "And you're the one that writes every word with me in spirit."

A smile blooms across her face. "I knew it was fate for us to meet."

Normally, I would have rolled my eyes, but now I'm starting to believe in fate a little bit, too. "Yeah. I think you're right."

Somehow, we found each other—an ocean apart for most of our lives. It feels like she has always known me, and I have always known her.

It's her turn to unzip her backpack. "In honor of this very special day, I have a surprise for you."

I lift my eyebrows. A surprise?

She reaches in and pulls out the starry blanket she bought that day at Chợ Bến Thành. She presses the bundle into my hand, and I unwrap it, revealing a miniature telescope and a tripod.

"I know you love looking at the stars." She presses the telescope into my hands, its weight heavy just like my heart. "So this is for you."

I blink away the mistiness in my eyes and cradle the telescope in my hand. "Thank you." A single tear rolls down my cheek.

Vivi scoots closer and I hand her the telescope to attach to the tripod. She sets it down, motioning for me to look. I peer through the lens as excitement pounds in my ears. I can feel Ba with me, his hand ruffling my hair, encouraging me to tell him about the stars. But instead of twinkling lights, I only see gray clouds.

"We can't see through the Sài Gòn smog!" I burst out laughing.

"What!" Vivi gapes and yanks the telescope from my hand to check herself. "I can't believe this."

Still laughing, I loop my arms around her from behind and tuck my face in her hair.

"Thank you. This means a lot to me," I murmur. "This . . . reminds me of my dad. Watching stars. We used to do it a lot before he passed."

Vivi turns toward me and I burrow my head in her neck. She kisses my temple.

"I've always loved writing because of him," I whisper. "I write because it made me feel closer to him somehow. Like when we'd cook up blog posts at our kitchen table together."

Vivi glides her hand up and down my back. "You're so much like him," she breathes.

"Why do you say that?"

"You take after him—your passions, your hard work," she says immediately. "Like him, you put the people you love first . . . sometimes even before yourself."

"That's what being a good daughter is." I recite the mantra I've clung to for so long. The mantra I often tell myself to squash away any doubts, any bubbling selfishness. "I have to put family first."

She plucks a plumeria from the branch, bringing it to her nose. "But, Lan, flowers are meant to grow."

A scratchiness in my throat makes it difficult to swallow, and as I hold Vivi's gaze, I can feel all her sincerity.

"Did you know that seventy percent of orchids are epiphytes?"

"Epi—what?"

She laughs. "When I googled your name, I learned that orchids are epiphytes. They grow attached to other plants, but not like a parasite. And before you tease me for being nerdy about this, I promise my long metaphor has a point. They're not anchored to the ground or to one specific nutrient source. They can get everything they need from the rain, air, and debris. They live in every habitat in the world except glaciers. You don't have to be rooted to one thing, Lan. You can adapt. You can bloom."

"What if I hurt the people I love? What if I never bloom?"

She wipes my tears with her sleeve, kissing the tearstains. We fall onto the picnic blanket, our legs intertwining, and my head in the crook of her neck. "You won't know unless you try. Do you . . . think you'll post more blogs again soon?"

I think of how within mere months, Vivi was able to get me to write again. Something I couldn't do myself. She's my lucky charm. What happens once she leaves? Will I stop writing again?

"I don't know." I tell her the truth. Maybe this story we've written together is the last thing I'll ever write. Maybe I can never write anything close to it.

"Take your time, Lan."

"What if it takes me decades before I can finally post something on my blog again?"

She snorts, and I join in her laughter, our voices echoing through the street. "I'll wait no matter how long you take. I'm your biggest fan. I'll take anything."

Tilting my head toward the sky, I breathe in the Sài Gòn air. Ba's favorite constellation, the Big Dipper, twinkles. Next to it is the Little Dipper—my favorite constellation. I used to tell him that as long as the Big and Little Dippers are together, me and him will be inseparable. Maybe Vivi is my North Star. Is this how Ba felt when I came into the world? When he told everyone that he found the brightest star? To me, she's brighter than all the stars in the universe.

I reread the story for the hundredth time, index finger hovering over the backspace button. Vivi swats my hand away. "Stop finding mistakes. This story is beautiful," she says.

I groan, throwing my arms up defensively. "I'm scared! What if there's a misplaced comma? What if they hate a sentence and throw away my application altogether? What about the subsections? Do they even make any sense?"

"Lan." She laces her hand through mine, an action so familiar to us now, but it still makes my heart skip with glee. "I know you're worried that the things we've written about city life and the people may sound boring, but the story sounds genuine. We talk about how hot and humid this city is, and how people's laughter makes the atmosphere seem cooler somehow. We describe the souls that live here, all the people that make Sài Gòn, Sài Gòn. Plus, with your background as a street food seller, we got to focus on the other side of tourism. The side we don't see often enough. We even included the flan lady, Bà Ngân, and Bác Tuấn—I like that our story portrays how everyone in this country is so strong. Always surviving and fighting no matter how hard it gets.

This story, at its heart, is about the beauty of Sài Gòn and the people living in it."

Together with Vivi next to me, I open the tab of the journalism contest and with all the bravery I could ever muster, I click the big, blue button.

Your application has been received.

Chapter Twenty-Six

VIVI

I wave goodbye to Lan and watch her back disappear into the dark before lifting a finger to my lips, a tingling sensation coursing through me as I replay our moments on that small rooftop overlooking Sài Gòn. It felt like the city was ours—like we could do anything and be all right. I wish I could take a photograph of that moment, of the feelings that fill me when I look at her, and frame it forever in my mind.

Instead of walking to my room, my legs drag me toward the kitchen and into the backyard where Bà Hai's hunching over a hearth and roasting some squids.

"Bà Hai?"

Surprised, she turns toward me with a burnt piece sticking out of her mouth. It seems tough, already giving me a toothache just from looking at it. "Vivi? You're still awake? What are you doing up so late?"

I smile sheepishly. "I could ask you the same thing. I just got back and saw that the kitchen lights were on. What are you doing?"

She returns the smile, fanning herself from the heat of the fire.

Grabbing a cup of water, she motions for me to come over. I tiptoe toward the backyard, the smoke from the hearth curling around us and into the night sky, fleeing into Sài Gòn's humidity.

"Here, sit with me." She nudges pieces of dry squid into my palm while popping one into her own mouth. "Eat some dry squid."

I smile softly, tearing the squid into bite-size pieces and hovering them over the fire. The flames crackle and the cool breeze tickles our backs. Bà Hai throws more coal into the fire. It hisses back at us, making me flinch, and she laughs.

"It's tasty," I say.

"Eating it at night like this reminds me of my days back in Hà Giang, when my family would squat around a fire, roasting sweet potatoes from the fields and fish from the nearby rivers."

"I didn't know you're from Hà Giang."

She chuckles and moves the logs around, making the fire dance back and forth. "Really? You can't tell from my northern accent?"

I blush. It's something that I've always been embarrassed about. Another sign of being Vietnamese but not fully Vietnamese. "I can't tell accents apart in general," I mumble shyly.

She laughs harder. "I'm only teasing." She clicks her tongue. "Too bad I don't have any sweet potatoes lying around."

"Tell me about Hà Giang," I ask. "What was it like?"

"Hà Giang was beautiful. The mountains were vast and stretching as high as the sky, as if they were actually steps to Heaven. In Hà Giang's province, there is also Quản Bạ, or Heaven's Gate. And from Heaven's Gate, you can see all the mountains, the open fields, and the rice paddies that gave us our life. But it wasn't always like that," Bà Hai says, a look of longing in her face as she tends the roasted squid, probably imagining herself decades ago when she was just a little girl.

"What do you mean?"

"Con, you ask many questions."

Laughing at my embarrassment, she continues. "It's a good thing to be curious. You must enjoy your youth. But, from the stories of my family, life was hard in Hà Giang during the French occupation of Việt Nam. And it wasn't just the French. The Japanese came, too, and they were just as ruthless as the French."

"How did . . . your family do it? Survive through all that?"

She shrugs. "They did everything they could—found any jobs they could get, traded everything for food. By some miracle, they lived and I came into this world. But con, a life in Việt Nam was still so hard for many of us."

"Did you . . . have to leave Hà Giang?" I ask the question I can already sense the answer to. I try to imagine that feeling, the sadness that would grip me if I were forced to leave Little Saigon and the only home I'd ever known.

"I was just a small child, but we left Hà Giang for Hà Nội, never looking back at the mountains and hills again."

I reach out to squeeze her hand, the hissing of the fire filling the silence between us. Like my parents, Bà Hai was forced to leave a home she has always known—a place she clearly loved.

A lump forms in my throat. "I'm sorry. Was it better to live in Hà Nội?"

Still staring into the fire, she only nods. "We tried finding work in Hà Nội, waiting tables, or working for someone—anything to feed ourselves. But when the Americans came to Việt Nam, rain turned into bombs—which meant death." Her voice cracks, and she lifts her hand to wipe away a tear.

"So, so many deaths," she continues. "To the point that none of us could go to school anymore because who knows what would happen during school? What if one day, the bombs came while I was at school and I never saw my family again?"

"But Việt Nam won, right?" Something good happened. The country survived.

Bà Hai doesn't respond. She continues staring at the hearth, still tossing leftover squid into the fire. She turns to me, her eyes glossy. "It's not black and white. It never is. The war wasn't just about winning or losing. It was us shouting at the world that we, too, are human."

"How could it not be about winning or losing, when so much was at stake?"

"Con, if there is one thing about war that I've learned, it is that it takes and takes and takes, relentlessly, without mercy. Vietnamese people are the ones that suffered the most—no matter which side of the war they were on. On both sides—in fact, on all sides—the war took everything away from all of us. People left Việt Nam, fleeing to wherever they could."

I suck in a breath. Bà Hai's comments remind me of Mom. I think of her living with the aftermath of a war, and how different Sài Gòn was from the city I'm visiting now.

Bà Hai speaks again. "We were like puppets, forced to fight among ourselves while the world watched and laughed without a care in the world. Without a care that we were bleeding our own land dry."

"I wish I had learned about this when I was growing up from my own parents. That they'd told me their stories. I never met my family here in Sài Gòn. I never knew what kind of people they were, and I felt like I missed out on such a big part of my own life."

Looking into the fire, I see the history of Việt Nam the way I learned it as a kid in the States—as something insignificant and small, not worth being included in every high school curriculum. Even movies and media only depict Việt Nam as a war-torn place, a country that needed saving. They hardly touch on the atrocities that happened here or the boat people who braved the seas. For all their puppetry, we're forgotten, our stories untold.

Bà Hai continues. "Hurt and loss take up so much space in our hearts—and they turn into hate. My husband's father was sent to reeducation camp after the war ended for being on the American side. Two weeks later, my mom and I received news that my brother on the Northern side was never going to return home because he died on the battlefield."

I say nothing, allowing the trickle of my tears to fall, staining my cheeks as I picture my own family tossed around in this war, facing horrors from all sides. Maybe Dad is right, that I can't blame Mom for wanting to avoid talking about all the hurt and loss. Maybe Bà Hai is right, that the scars run too deep, that they're too agonizing to face. Perhaps there isn't a right and a wrong and a good and a bad and a truth and a lie . . . There are too many perspectives, too many personal losses and sacrifices and griefs to try to quantify what happened in Việt Nam into something simple, something people can learn for five minutes in history classes.

"But despite everything, we're still all Vietnamese," she continues. "And do you know what that means?"

I shake my head. "No."

"When you're Vietnamese, you have tenacity in your blood. You have the will to survive. So no matter what, we will always be okay, because we're Vietnamese."

Chapter Twenty-Seven

LAN

"What are you looking at?" I ask Vivi, whose eyes are planted on the sky-line in the distance. Behind us are noisy street food stalls, and the smell of bánh bột chiên makes me salivate.

"Just the city," she says. Rowdy students bump into our table, apologizing before scurrying away.

My hand glides up and down her back, and I can feel her shivering slightly beneath my fingertips. "What about the city?"

"I keep thinking of Sài Gòn from decades ago—about what you and everyone else has told me about how different life was back then. All this time, I've been falling in love with the Sài Gòn that's in front of us, and I didn't think about the Sài Gòn that existed before I was born. The Sài Gòn my mom lived in."

I sigh, understanding Vivi perfectly—the war. Although the war ended more than fifty years ago, and she and I weren't even born yet, its ghost still haunts us today. I think about Má, about how she lived in the wake of a country recovering from war. Like her, most people living in this city still carry the scars from those days, even the people with us on this very street.

"Do you think . . . that's why your mom left?"

She sighs. "I don't know—and I'm not sure if I'll find the answer when we visit my family tomorrow. From being here, *living* here, I'm learning that sometimes, people have reasons to leave the place they've always loved."

Her words squeeze my chest, and the dream of getting outside of Sài Gòn returns. But I also think about Triết, about how he left his Bến Tre for this city, and my great-grandma, finding a home in Sài Gòn as an immigrant. "Maybe being in America takes away some of that pain, when you're so far from home that the pain doesn't hurt as much anymore."

"How did my parents do it? How did they make a new home in a completely strange place? With all the insults that have been thrown our way and how we were never seen as American enough—no matter how hard we tried to be like them—my parents never looked back. If my mom ever felt homesick or out of place, she never wore it on her face, at least not in front of me."

I look back at the skyline, and the heart of Sài Gòn stares back at me, neon lights dancing across the river. Landmark 81, Việt Nam's tallest building and the world's seventeenth tallest building, glows so brightly that it seems to set the city ablaze. It makes me feel so small. "Maybe they never looked back because of you—because they have you. You're their reason to get up every day and to survive." It's what Má is to me. She's my reason to keep going.

"But I didn't ask for that."

"Maybe it's not you . . . but it's your mom wanting to give you the world, to protect you, because you're the only one she has." The words fly out of my mouth, feelings I've been repressing so long—things I wish I could say to Má every time she reminds me that I shouldn't need to work so hard for her.

She sighs. "What if I don't need protecting?"

"But that's what we do for our family—we protect them from things that could potentially hurt them."

"I just . . . I just want to know. I don't want my mom to baby me and *protect* me anymore. Whatever she's faced, I'm ready for it."

I put down my chopsticks, the bột chiên overwhelmingly sour on my tongue now. "What if your mom never meant to hurt you? What if she's only doing what she knows might be best?"

"What's best for my mom isn't always what's best for me."

I let those words hang between us, but my thoughts return to Má once again. Do *I*, her daughter, know what's best for Ma? Am I hurting her by protecting her with everything I've got?

"Will you be okay tomorrow?" I ask Vivi.

She nods. "As okay as I'll ever be when meeting a family I've never known."

Chapter Twenty-Eight

VIVI

District 2 is separated from District 1 by the Sài Gòn River. As we cross under Cầu Ba Son, or the Thủ Thiêm 2 Bridge, I can't help but stare at downtown Sài Gòn from the motorbike—the receding financial towers and all the high-rise buildings, where my story in Sài Gòn began— as the residential areas of District 2 loom in the distance.

"I wish my mom was here." It feels weird, meeting my family for the first time without the one person who should be with me.

Lan sighs, and I can feel her breathing with my arms wrapped tightly around her waist. "If you don't find them, it won't be the worst thing. You still have family. Your parents."

My chest tightens. Sometimes I wonder if Lan thinks I'm a brat for trying so hard. If she thinks I'm ungrateful. She cares, and I know that, but sometimes I can't help but wish that she'd see what I'm doing is as important as the contest, too.

"I guess you're right."

Now that we've crossed into District 2, it feels like we're in a familiar yet different world. The tall skyline is replaced by smaller homes, yet the streets are crowded nonetheless. Houses in various colors and styles stare at us as we pass. Some are polished white while others look older, decorated by years of weather in Sài Gòn. Mini-marts are on every corner, squished side by side with endless rows of buildings. Shopkeepers squat on their mini stools and watch as their customers pour in just in time for lunch. Dogs and cats wander through the streets. The smell of fried bananas wafts through the air, making my stomach rumble.

We turn into an alleyway, driving toward the cathedral from the photograph and the one Bác Tuấn spoke of.

We stop in front of a fruit stand, with layers and layers of colorful fruits stacked on top of each other. The prices are incomparable to California—barely a dollar for a cup filled to the brim with jackfruit, rambutan, and young coconut meat. One of these in Little Saigon would cost at least ten dollars, and yet Mom would always bring them home, and we'd sit on the couch sharing the small bites between us. It was one of the only times she would talk about Việt Nam. She'd let it slip that these fruits are from her home, where the weather is hotter and the sky a little brighter, and the climate allows for these trees to grow. I pull out the photo of Mom in front of that church and look up at the building right in front of me, imagining her here. She was so young. Like me.

Lan turns to the young girl working at the fruit stand and says something in Vietnamese. My heart pounds in my ears. What if this stranger doesn't know my family? What if they've moved out of District 2? And if they do know—will I finally get to meet the family I've never known? What about *Mom*; how do I even bring this up to her?

My fate rests in the hands of a simple answer from a stranger, and that's terrifying.

The girl looks at the photo, and I can see recognition on her face. "You said you're looking for Hiền?" she asks in Vietnamese.

We nod, and she signals for us to wait before bringing out an older lady, and my heart almost drops when I see her face. It's like seeing the spitting image of Mom. But the feeling seems mutual, because the woman looks shocked to see me—and suddenly, the feeling like I don't belong comes creeping back. Like maybe I shouldn't have come, shouldn't have tried.

Still, I know for a fact that I'm finally staring at Mom's sister. My *aunt*.

"Xin chào." I try my best to not butcher the pronunciations. "Co ten la Hiền—"

The woman stops me before I can finish asking if she's actually Hiền, and with teary eyes, pulls me into a hug. "Hoa oi, em về lúc nào?"

My body tenses, my arms go limp, and I don't know what to do. How do I respond to that question? To Mom's sister calling me by Mom's name, and asking me when I had returned? How do I tell this lady that I'm not Mom? How do I tell her that her sister isn't here?

She pulls away before I can say anything and examines my face. "À, con không phải Hoa! Cô xin lỗi."

You're not Hoa. My heart drops at her apology and how naturally she says *Hoa*—how that name has always felt important to her. It's a strange thing to be mistaken for Mom, especially when I've always seen us as two different people, leading two different lives. But here, in Sài Gòn, our lives intersect, and suddenly I can imagine the younger version of Mom right next to me, hugging the sister she left.

I fish for my wallet, my heart pounding. Placing the photo in her hand, I repeat the phrase I had Lan help me memorize and practice aloud. "Cô có biết những người này không?"

The question that I've been asking ever since I got to Việt Nam: *Do you know who these people are?* And somehow, after all the markets and street food stalls and motorbike rides, I'm here. I'm standing in front of my aunt. The family I never knew about.

She continues staring at the photo, not saying a word. "Who . . . How you get this?" She switches to English, sensing my American accent coming through. "Hoa . . . con gái của Hoa?"

I swallow, meeting her gaze. "Yes, I'm Hoa's daughter."

She takes a step forward and looks closely at my face. "You look like Hoa."

Not knowing what to do, I just stare into her eyes. They are wide, with creasing at the top of her eyelids, while her eyebrows are sparse and thin. Just like Mom's. "Con, do you want to come with me?" she asks in Vietnamese.

I look at Lan nervously, but she motions for me to go ahead with my aunt. "It'll be okay. You got this," she says.

I nod. "Thanks for bringing me here. And thanks for everything you've done for me up until now."

"I'll pick you up?"

I nod, my heart swelling with warmth for her. Despite all the anxieties and hurt, she's been the one constant for me all throughout Sài Gòn. "Yeah."

Aunt Hiển leads me into a small alley diagonal to the fruit stand, her hand on my back as we walk. It reminds me of Mom, and the way she'd do the same when we'd walk side by side in the Vietnamese grocery store in Little Saigon. Within seconds, Mom's childhood home comes into view. It's a two-story building tucked away in the heart of District 2, overlooking a quaint courtyard that contains a banana tree and an herb garden in a tub. There's a balcony with a clothing rack, and the clothes on it sway softly in the wind. I can hear children laughing in the house. It shows signs of being lived in, of stories being exchanged, and of memories shared between families.

I have an odd feeling that I'm intruding. Like I don't belong. Though we're technically family, they're strangers to me as much as I am to them. The inside of the house is decorated with colorful tiled patterns of flowers, wooden chairs and desks, a TV in the middle with children's toys next to it, and straw mats on the floor. The space isn't wide but long and tall, and the furniture is stacked to the side to make space for other things. I see several altars as I walk by, incense burning, and flowers placed next to them. There's a staircase by the entrance, and I linger as Aunt Hiền walks ahead, my eyes finding the puzzle pieces I've been looking for my entire life.

The walls are filled with photos of Mom. She is everywhere.

"Con," Aunt Hiền speaks again, and I look up to find her carrying a photo album in her arms. "Do you want to take a look?"

Mom. Pictures of Mom. Photos I hadn't ever seen before, and it just hits me then that I've seen never Mom younger than my age. And as I sit here, my eyes glued to the roundness of her cheeks and how her eyes kiss in the corners just like mine, I'm unable to separate my own face from hers. It's like staring into a mirror, but this time, it's also a time portal. A key to unlocking Mom's life in Sài Gòn.

I skim my fingers over each page, my thoughts a jumbled mess as I flip through the timeline of Mom's life in front of me: Mom in Grandma's arms as a baby, Mom taking her first steps as a toddler, Mom and Aunt Hiền in front of this very house, Mom in a high school uniform, Mom and Grandma surrounded by Trung Thu lanterns. This entire trip, *everything* I have been doing, I've been following in Mom's footsteps without knowing it.

A photo falls out of the album and surprise overtakes me when I see the faces in it: Mom and . . . a boy? They're standing in front of an alley with street food stalls behind them, and I recognize her outfit from another photo I took from her drawer. The boy has a goofy smile, they're standing next to each other under a hoa phượng tree with Mom in a white áo dài, and suddenly I can see it: Mom running through Sài Gòn with this same boy and him photographing her laugh.

I turn the page and find an empty spot in the album, right next to a photo of Mom and Aunt Hiền in front of Chợ Bến Thành. I pull the photo I stole from Mom's closet out of my pocket, the one of her, Aunt Hiền, and Grandma in front of the same marketplace. All this time, Mom's been holding on to her own memory of this very moment. This was when it had ended, the last time they all took a picture together, and the last photo of Mom in Sài Gòn.

I turn to Aunt Hiền and ask the question that's been burning in my throat. "Did you know about me?"

She looks at me sadly, and I already know the answer from her face. Still, the shaking of her head confirms it—and I don't know which hurts more, the fact that Mom didn't care to tell her family about me, or the fact that my family never knew I existed at all.

"But I knew when I saw you," Aunt Hiền says. "The moment I looked at you—I knew who you were. I just wish my sister told me, too."

"Have you . . . kept in touch with her?"

"In a way, yes."

Aunt Hiền shuffles through a few envelopes before pulling out white, almost yellowing ones. They were sent by Mom, with our return address on the back. The contents of each is the same: statements of confirmation from banks. Mom's been wiring them money since she's been in California. There are no notes, no heartfelt letters. Only a single sentence:

Chi, I hope this is enough for you and Ma.

And as I go through the envelopes, I can see the amount of money increasing each month. The most recent statement was last month's. All this time, I never knew.

None of this makes any sense. The money, the secrecy, *Mom.*

Somehow, I found everything but also nothing. It seems Mom has shut everyone out of her past and present. We were never meant to meet, and if it weren't for this trip—if it weren't for *Lan*—I still wouldn't know my family existed.

"Hoa à? Con về nhà à?" A weak voice floats through the emptiness, and my heart drops when I realize what the question meant. Someone in this house, someone who loves Mom, is asking for her—asking if she has come back.

Aunt Hiền turns her head to the corridor. "Do you want to meet your grandma?"

I wonder if normal kids get asked that question. Steadying my breath, I pick at my cuticles and nod. We stop in front of a small room with a pale blue door, the color mismatched against the dusty green of the walls.

Aunt Hiền opens the door and touches my shoulder. "Just so you know, she can't talk much."

A shaky voice calls out from the corner of the room. Her voice is a deep rumble, both breathy and . . . sorrowful. "Is that Hoa?"

Blinking to adjust my eyes to the dimness of the room, I look at the elderly lady resting on the pile of pillows. She looks just like Mom but much frailer. I wonder if Mom knows that her mother is bedridden and calling for her daughter.

"Bà Ngoại?" I murmur back, fully aware of the darkness of the room and how quiet it is. In Vietnamese, *Bà Ngoại* means "grandma from your mom's side," and ever since I learned the word in Vietnamese class, I've always wondered if I would ever say it outside of the classroom.

She speaks in a whisper so low I would have missed it if I wasn't holding my breath. "Hoa? You've come back? I'm so sorry, my baby. My Hoa."

My heart tightens and I clench my fists. My own grandmother can't recognize me, only her daughter. The daughter that left her.

Aunt Hiền hurries over to Bà Ngoại's side and straightens her pillows. "She's not doing well today. Please don't mind her."

Biting my lips, I glance around the room. It's full of pictures of my mother and aunt. In every photo with Bà Ngoại, my mom holds fake flower props—some behind her ears, some placed prettily on her lap like a bouquet.

I walk toward my grandma and sit on the chair next to her bed. I study her face, seeing some of my own features. I take her hand and smooth the wrinkles on her palm. Bà Ngoại locks her fingers with mine and holds my hand delicately, as if I might disappear at any moment. As if I'm a flower about to leave with the wind.

"Bà Ngoại, I'm Vivian. I'm so happy to see you," I tell her earnestly in Vietnamese.

"Hoa, con ơi." The shakiness of her voice breaks into a sob. "You stupid, stupid girl. Why did you have to go? Why did you have to follow that boy? Why did you leave your mother?"

Aunt Hiền sucks in a breath behind me before grabbing my arm and nudging me toward the door.

Still, Bà Ngoại continues, her voice rising. "Stupid girl! Your mother is dying! Do you not have shame? No love left for your mother? All I want . . ." Her body convulses, her shoulders folding into themselves. "All I want is to see your face again. Hoa ơi, Má thương con."

As Aunt Hiền leads me out of the room, I begin to understand that love contradicts. That when you have an overwhelming amount of love for someone, you can hurt them, too.

Chapter Twenty-Nine

LAN

Vivi doesn't talk the entire ride home. In fact, she doesn't talk at all when we step inside her dormitory, either. Her eyes are sad, and my heart hurts as I reach toward her before her lips crash onto mine, and we stumble against the hallway of the dorm, her body pinning me to the wall. She dips her head, her mouth refusing to leave mine as her grip on my arms tightens. Heat dances in my stomach, but I can't shake off the feeling that something's wrong. All the giddiness evaporates, leaving me with all of Vivi's hurt.

"Vivi." I break apart from her lips, my breathing ragged. "What's wrong?"

She doesn't say anything and just takes my hand. I let her, my palm touching the softness of her cheeks. I wish I could undo all this hurt—all these negative feelings—make them deflate somehow.

"Sometimes," she starts. "Sometimes I wish I could do *more*. I wish I could just snap my fingers and solve everything that's been making me feel this way."

Little does she know I feel the exact same way about her. How I desperately wish I could magic away all the pain she's bottling inside.

"All these emotions inside me, I'm still trying to make sense of what they are," she continues. "I don't know how to feel. I'm angry, but I'm also sad. Then seconds later, I'm confused. And even after all this, after finding my family, I have more questions than answers."

"Tell me about it. Take your time." I tighten my embrace around Vivi, wiping her tearstained face with the sleeves of my shirt. Minutes pass, and we stay like that until her sobs slow down and her breathing calms and she can stand again.

"My mom kept all of this from me. The fact that I have an aunt and a grandma—a family here. But you know what's even worse? She never told them I exist, either."

There's an overwhelming urge in me to absorb all of Vivi's sadness for her, to somehow and someway make her smile again. "So they . . . didn't know who you were."

She nods. "I saw another photo of her I've never seen before. One of my mom next to a boy. She looks . . . in love. Just how many secrets is my mom hiding from me, Lan? How many things has she kept only to herself?"

"Do you not recognize the boy?"

She shakes her head. "No. He's not my dad. But I think . . . she came to America with him."

"Oh."

"My grandma and my mom," she continues. "I don't think they had the best relationship, and I don't think Sài Gòn was a thriving city back then, especially when she was a kid after the war."

"It wasn't," I say, thinking of all the stories Ba told me. "People did everything they could to survive before we were born. Families were torn apart and hundreds of thousands of people left Việt Nam."

She swallows. "And my mom was one of them . . ."

"But your mom's family stayed."

She nods. "My grandma is sick. She thought I was my mom, so while I was with her, she kept calling out my mom's name. Sometimes, she'd yell at her and other times, she'd cry about how much she misses her. But over and over, she kept asking why my mom left, why she left Việt Nam with a boy."

"Do you think she ran away with someone?"

"I don't know, but I can't imagine my mom doing that. She's always been so . . . independent? And she's never talked about this boy. Ever."

I chew on my lip, my heart still hurting for Vivi. "Maybe . . . he's someone she doesn't want you to know about."

She sighs. "Another secret. How many does my mom have? Part of me wishes I could stay here forever with you and not have to face her when I get home."

"But you don't want that." I say the very thing that's been weighing on me these days. The fact that Vivi is leaving soon. "You want to fix this for your family. For you."

She swallows, nodding limply. "I do. It's no longer just my mom's secrets and past, it's *mine* too. I want my mom to look at me, really look at me, and tell me where it all went wrong. Why she chose to become a boat person and a refugee and trade her life here for another hard life in the States."

"I admire you, Vivi," I say earnestly. "You flew across an entire ocean because you knew deep down that learning about your family and Việt Nam is important to you. You don't avoid the truth even if it scares you. I know nothing makes sense right now and you don't know what to do, but just the fact that you did all this . . . that's really brave."

And more than I could ever do.

"Is it really bravery? I'm ashamed—this entire semester, this feeling that I've done nothing but lying has been haunting me."

"You had to do what you felt was right, and it led you here to Sài Gòn. Do you . . . regret coming?"

I don't need to hear her answer—I already know it—but still, she says, "No. I've never regretted this trip, this decision to come here, one bit. I just—I don't know where to go from here. I'm not sure how I can stitch things back together anymore."

She exhales softly. "I just want to understand my mom. I think that's all this is, the cumulation of this trip, the family in Việt Nam, and her life that she's never once talked about. I just want to hear her voice telling me why she left . . . why she never told me about it."

I gulp. "What about . . . asking her directly? You've got all the answers you can find here—there's one person left to ask."

"I think that's the worst part, that no matter how much I try and how far I've come to find the answers, it all circles back to my mom."

"Maybe she'll understand this time. Maybe she'll finally see where you are coming from."

"Do you really think so?"

"If anyone can do it, it's you, Vivi."

Chapter Thirty

VIVI

I work up the courage, bile rising in my throat as I stare at Mom's contact in my phone. I've had her number memorized since grade school, and dialing it always felt so comforting. Not anymore.

I hear her pick up. "A-lô? Vivi?"

I clear my throat, trying to steady my breathing. "Hi, Mom. Can I talk to you?"

"Yes, con. You can always talk to Mommy. What do you need?"

"Mom . . . about the photos you've been looking for—"

"Don't worry about them," she cuts me off. "I'll be okay. I'm sure they'll turn up soon."

Guilt overwhelms me. I know she's lying. I wonder how many times she's had to lie to me like this before. "I know where the photos are. They're with me."

She inhales sharply. "What? Con, why do you have them?"

"Because . . . I'm in Việt Nam, Mom." I can feel the line going cold—can picture her face, a cross between anger and disappointment.

"I haven't been in Singapore this entire time. I'm in Sài Gòn. Your home. I wanted to come here because—"

She refuses to listen, her voice rising as she speaks. "How could you lie to me like this? Why did you go to Việt Nam without telling me?"

"Mom—I—I can explain."

"How could you!" she practically screams through the phone. "Vivi, I have told you many, many times that Sài Gòn is dangerous. Con, you are so reckless . . . you *lied* to me!"

"Mom, I'm fine!" I protest. There's no point arguing back. I'll just let her know I'm physically healthy and end the conversation. "I really am. I made friends in Sài Gòn. I promise, Mom, this city is so beautiful and you have nothing to worry about."

"Do I know these friends?" she presses further.

"No, but that's not the point—"

"I raised you better!" I can hear Dad's voice in the background trying to calm her. "Now you're running around in Việt Nam by yourself. You know they can hurt you? What if Mommy won't see you again?"

"Mom!" I sigh with all the teenage angst rising in my throat. "Stop it, please. Stop acting like I'll get kidnapped and trafficked. I'm safe!"

"You lied to Mommy, con. I can't believe this. You never listen to Mommy."

I blink, tears falling down my cheeks. "Mom, I know about Aunt Hiền and Bà Ngoại."

The line goes dead silent.

"What are you talking about?"

"Stop lying to me, Mom. We've had family here all this time and you never told me about it. You didn't even tell them about *me*."

"You lied to me."

Frustration grips me. "Mom, can you *please* stop focusing on the fact that I lied to you about Việt Nam and start focusing on the fact that *you* have been lying, too?"

"I didn't lie. It's better that con didn't know."

Great. Just great. "Well, I know now, Mom." My voice cracks. "You never wanted to come back, because something happened, and you ran away. I know about your childhood home, about how you left Việt Nam when you were my age, and the fruit stand that Aunt Hiền runs. I even know about the boy in the photo—"

"You don't know anything about Mommy. You think you do, but you don't."

"Then tell me."

"You wouldn't understand."

"Wouldn't understand? How would I understand when you haven't even tried telling me?" I want to give up, anger boiling within me. All the rage from my childhood, from being excluded from our family history, from seeing my aunt and grandma comes spilling out. It pours and pours out of me.

"All my life, you never wanted to talk about Việt Nam, even when I asked. How could you have kept *our family* from me? How could you walk away from the people you love and pretend they don't exist? Grandma is *dying*, Mom—did you know that? I wasn't going to meet my own grandma if you had continued to *lie* to me. If you cared, you'd come. You'd be back here, too."

She sucks in a breath, and I know I've crossed a line I can never turn back from.

Finally, Mom clears her throat, her voice shaky. "Some things cannot be said, and con, you know better than to ask."

"You can't expect that of me," I say through clenched teeth.

"I can because you're my daughter." With that, she ends the phone call, leaving me in tears with an aching pain in my heart.

I stare at the blank screen, tempted to fling my phone on the concrete floor and scream. Scream about my mom, her expectations, and the unsaid words between us. But I don't, and instead, I resign myself to sobbing on my mattress, arms cradling my own face as hot tears blur my vision and stain my shirt.

My phone buzzes again. A text from Lan.

The journalism results are in. They just emailed me. Can you please come over?

Chapter Thirty-One

LAN

"Over here!" I yell when I catch sight of a breathless Vivi running toward me, her sandals squeaking as she makes her way from the front gate to the house.

"Hey," she says, her hand reaching for mine, and though there's a smile on her face, I can sense something is wrong. Still, she doesn't let me get a word in, and scoots my butt to the left of the swing as she takes the phone from me. "Are you nervous?"

"I'm terrified." I stare at my hands, fingers itching to pick at my scabs. Anything to pass time. To subdue the rising anxiety. "This is all or nothing, Vivi. I need to win. My family needs the money."

"I'm confident they chose you. It will all work out. I promise."

"Can you open it for me? I've been staring at the unread email for the past fifteen minutes, and I just can't do it."

What if they say no?

What if this was all for nothing?

What if despite all our efforts, there was no hope anyway?

Vivi inhales sharply, her nails rapping against my phone as she clears her throat. "'Dear Miss Phan Ngọc Lan, thank you for your submission to the *Southeast Asia Travel Magazine*. The team was completely struck by your writing and poise, and by how you eloquently described Sài Gòn. We could feel the deep love you have for the city, as well as how much cultural knowledge you harbor. Unfortunately . . .'" Her face falls.

"What?" I try to pry for my phone, but she yanks her arm away.

She chews on her bottom lip, her eyes darting back and forth from me to my phone screen. "Do you want me to read the rest?"

I nod.

"Unfortunately, we ultimately decided to move on with another story for the contest."

A breath hitches in my throat, the whistling in my ears becoming louder. "Oh."

It's over.

I didn't win.

I couldn't do it.

"Wait. There's more." She grabs my arm. "However, we truly did fall in love with your writing and portrayal of Vietnam. We'd love to offer you one of the newest positions on our team. An opportunity as a paid journalist throughout Southeast Asia writing content for the magazine."

Eyes wide, Vivi grabs both of my shoulders and envelops me into a full hug. "Lan! This is huge. You didn't win, but you kind of did? They gave you a *job*. You can *travel*!" Still beaming, she squeezes my hands. "I told you. Didn't I? I knew you could do it."

I avoid her gaze. Tears prick at the corners of my eyes. They're not happy tears. Instead, I feel . . . angry.

She blinks and hesitates. "Is there something wrong?"

Too many things are wrong. I'm confused about my own emotions. I should be happy, so why aren't I?

"I don't think I can take the job."

She frowns, my answer catching her off guard. Hurt forms on her face, and still holding my hand, she fumbles through her words, her voice cracking. "But why not? You want to go see the world. To travel and learn and grow. Now you can! You can do what you've always dreamed of. If you have a good paying job," she continues. "Wouldn't you be able to send money back? That was your goal, right? The money. It's not like you're leaving for good. You can always visit."

"You don't understand, Vivi."

What if something happens while I'm away? What if I never get the chance to say goodbye again?

Tears well up in her eyes. "Don't say that. Don't say that to *me*. At least help me understand rather than just brushing me off! My own mom says that to me, but how am I supposed to understand when all people do is lie and *not tell me anything*?"

I dig my nails into my palm, prickling my skin, but they remind me not to cry. "I can't change overnight. I can't abandon this entire city and my family. I can't just get up and leave for an 'opportunity.'"

Her lips quiver as her temple scrunches, and my heart drops at the tears forming in her eyes. "I'm not expecting you to change. I'm encouraging you to put yourself first."

The ache in my temple pounds relentlessly and I furrow my brows, wincing at the pain. Can Vivi not understand that our lives are too different? Leaving Sài Gòn for a temporary job? That's a year or two without me at the stall. I can't do that to Má.

"Don't you think that I want to? Every day I look at the tourists in the city and wish that I could be them. But I can't," I choke out. "I'm not *you*. I can't just go to another part of the world and play tourist. This city—this *life*—isn't just the idealized version you're seeing. It's real, and I have to live it. Those dreams about traveling outside of Sài Gòn? They are just that, dreams."

"All this time, you really thought that I was just playing tourist?"

"That's not what I mean—"

"I thought I felt safe with *you*, Lan. That for the first time ever, I found somewhere I feel like I can call home with you here. I thought, *finally*, someone understands me."

"Vivi, I can't just leave my mom! She's all I have left. I'm not lucky like you. I don't have both of my parents. I can't just get on a plane and go anywhere I want like you. I can't just lie to my parents about a study abroad program. I can't even go where my dad is anymore. I have people to take care of here. I have a *life* here."

She freezes, and I immediately regret what I just said.

"Vivi—"

She swallows, her shoulders convulsing. "No—you're right. I don't have a life here. I never really belonged. But I didn't know that's how you feel about me, too."

The ground spins beneath me, and I know I should say something, beg her for forgiveness, apologize about what came out of me, but instead, I'm rooted to where I am.

"Lan, I need to know, please tell me if that's what you really think of me."

I can't, can't even open my mouth. Because the truth is, I *do* envy Vivi and her life, with both parents and traveling outside of where she grew up and everything that's opposite of mine.

Her face searches for mine before contorting, and realization hits us both that I have nothing to say. She turns on her heel, and unlike when we first met, this time, she's the one running away from me—tears streaming down her cheeks.

My wobbly legs will my body inside, where I slide to the floor and clutch myself in a fetal position. My heart beats wildly, my palms sweaty as my eyes sting and, zeroing in on Ba's portrait on the altar, my mind begs him to tell me what to do.

The door slides open and Triết steps in. Frantic, I wipe my eyes with the sleeves of my hoodie. "Hey, why did your friend go running off like that—"

I hide my face from him, still clutching my small body together. I breathe in and out and count from one to ten. "Mind your own business, Triết."

Sighing, he sets down the bag of groceries and sits next to me. He unwraps one of the bags and hands me a bar of ice cream, coconut, and scoots closer to me, unwrapping his own ice cream bar. We eat together in silence.

Finding the silence unbearable for the first time in my life, I speak up. "I didn't win the contest. But they invited me to be a paid journalist instead. Which means . . . leaving."

Triết exhales deeply, his temple pinched. "When is it going to get through to you that maybe, just maybe, your mom doesn't expect anything of you? You've been holding on to this idea that you need to take care of her forever—by yourself."

I bite my tongue, holding back on the harsh words that threaten to spill out. Triết means well, he does. But he doesn't understand the pain of losing a parent.

"You think that I don't know how you feel and that's why you're giving me that look." He laughs. "Do you know why I left Bến Tre? Why I never really visit?"

The remaining ice cream turns sour on my tongue. "What? Why?"

"My dad always said that since I'm the only male in the family, I need to inherit his land. Growing up, I hated it. I hated farming, I was always more interested in drawings and sketches and seeing how people can build things. All my sisters are good at all this agricultural stuff, and they have the passion for it. But when I asked for my dad's permission to come here to study and told him that I want something different for myself, he threw all my clothes and belongings out into the front yard. He disowned me. So I left, and I found a new family here."

"You never told me about this."

He shrugs, playing with his hands on his lap. "I didn't know what to say . . . you know how it is—the burden of being a loyal child to your parents. I had a lot of guilt, and a lot of shame, too. Your mom knew, or at least she sensed something was up, but she said nothing and took me in like a son. Lan, I may not know how it feels to lose someone that I love, but I do know the painful rift between a child and their parent, and I don't want to see you and your mom like this anymore. Talk to her, she just wants the best for you. Stop carrying all that burden by yourself. Let your mom fly a bit, too; don't let your dad's memory overshadow your own life."

A painful sob escapes me. It's not like I haven't thought about all these things that he's accusing me of. "How can I even learn to live, Triết? When it feels even more painful every single day without my dad? I broke my promise to him. I didn't pick up his call that day. If I did, he wouldn't have pushed himself to drive back alone sick. If I had answered, he'd still be here."

I failed him. He never came back because of *me*.

"I can't answer these questions for you, Lan."

I'm tired. So tired of people telling me that they can't tell me what to do. Life would be so much easier that way. I don't know what I want, and I certainly don't know what Ba would have wanted.

I start crying again, and Triết hands me more napkins. "It's okay," he says softly. "It's not your fault. You can't live with this guilt for the rest of your life."

"I don't know what to do," I whisper. "I'm scared."

He strokes my hair and I stare at the Popsicle stick I dropped on the floor. I look just like it—frail and ready to snap if someone just bends me a little.

A memory of Ba flashes through me. We were at the top of the hill, about to test run our paper kite. I was so scared to run down with him. *Be brave, my little flower! I am always with you!*

Willing the memory to dissipate, I squeeze my eyes shut and sob harder into Triết's pillow, letting him run his fingers through my hair, comforting me. The pillowcase is damp from my sweat, my hair tangled in knots, and my forehead sticky to the touch. Triết doesn't care, just letting me sob until my throat is dry and my nostrils feel raw.

The door to the house creaks and Má's footsteps approach us. She stops short in front of me, looking down at me with her soft eyes. She and Triết whisper back and forth, causing my chest to tighten even more. Ushering Triết away, she takes his place next to me, sweeping the tangled hair from my face.

She takes my face into her arms, cradling me tenderly like she always did when I was young. The simple act brings more tears into my eyes. I didn't know I missed her warmth this much.

"Why didn't you tell me about the contest?"

"I wasn't trying to keep it a secret from you, Má, I just . . . didn't know how to tell you. I . . . didn't want to fail you. Didn't want you to place your hopes in me only to be disappointed—like you are now."

In and out, in and out. I try to steady my breathing, yet my palms are now pools of sweat.

"Lan," Má says finally, her voice shaking. "You don't have to keep everything to yourself. You don't have to do everything by yourself for us."

My chest squeezes. Everything I've done has been for her. "I have to protect us. Protect our family. Protect you."

She gives me an exaggerated sigh. "Con, I just want you to be happy."

"I *am* happy."

She continues. "You know I would have let you go wherever it is that you want to, right? I would never force you to stay by my side."

Shame eats at me, and I find myself wanting to make myself smaller. Smaller and smaller until I disappear.

"Má," I sigh, not wanting to argue or fight anymore. "I don't want to be away from you."

As if my answer is ridiculous, she wrinkles her eyebrows. "I have Triết. He can help."

"I want to take care of you myself! Triết can help, but he can't do the things that I can. What if he doesn't know where you keep your medicine? What if something happens while I am away? What if he doesn't know where you are like I do?"

I look down at my hands, clutching them close to my heart. "I can't lose you, too."

Tears stream down my cheeks once again. "Ever since he left, I've lived every day trying to be your rock. Trying to protect you. I can't make the same mistake again."

Má shushes me before gathering me into her arms and stroking my hair, something that has always calmed me. Something she hasn't done since Ba passed.

"There are so many things that you can do without me, con. Without me holding you back. You were so busy looking after me and the shop that you didn't even take care of yourself. I know how you canceled your examination dates before you graduated. Your teacher told me that you didn't want to go to college. I told her that isn't my Lan at all. My daughter who pores over her books. My daughter who takes after her father's love for stories and words. There is not a single day that goes by that I don't wish to give you more than what we have. There's not a single day that I don't feel like I've failed you.

"With this job you've worked so hard for, you should be proud of yourself," she continues. "I don't care what you want to do, where you want to go. If you want to go to university, then do it. If you want to travel abroad and be a journalist, then do it. But do it for yourself. Pick the option that *you* want."

"But Má, what about you? What will you do when I'm not here?"

"Con, Má will be okay. I don't need you to worry about me. I have Triết, Chú Hai, the neighbors, and so many other people. I have so many people here. You have to realize that, Lan, that we are not alone. We have each other, but we also have the people that love us, too."

All this time, she has always wanted the best for me. She never wanted me to carry all this burden or to be her perfect daughter.

She brings me closer and kisses my head. I realize that she's right, that Chú Hai's right, and that Vivi's right. My heart aches for the girl that I love. I need to see Vivi. But not yet. Not tonight.

I was right, too. I know now it was right of me to protect Má, to rebuild this family. But Ba is not here anymore. I can't bring him back. I can only look forward.

"I'm proud of you, Lan, and I know your dad would be proud of you, too."

"Do you really think so?" I whisper.

"I do, con gái yêu của mẹ. I do."

Chapter Thirty-Two

VIVI

It doesn't get worse than this, than waking up the next morning with puffy eyes and the memories of what happened the day before, when the girl who means everything to you broke your heart. When everything shattered right before your eyes, and you don't know what to do except pick up the pieces of who you are now and try to not *think* about *her*.

And it doesn't get worse than fiddling with my phone all day with no energy to focus in class and all I think about is Mom, then Lan, then Mom, then Lan. I've gotten everything I've wanted from this trip, to learn about the Sài Gòn that Mom grew up in and to meet my favorite blogger—so how did it all go so, so wrong?

My eyes wander to the photo spread on my desk: All of Mom's photographs are now joined by pictures me and Lan took together. Mom in front of Chợ Bến Thành and right next to it a selfie of me and Lan by the market. Mom sitting on a blue plastic chair on the street, in her hand a bánh mì. Me, photographed by Lan, eating Bánh Mì 98.

Mom in an áo dài at a Trung Thu festival. Lan and I with the dancing lions at Trung Thu.

The noises from the street below pull me out of my thoughts, and as I stare at the Sài Gòn skyline through my window, I think about how I've grown so comfortable looking at it every day. How it's so hard to imagine being back in California.

How, as I fall asleep, I realize that all of this noise, this humidity, and the people will still be here as I *leave*. Everything will remain the same. People will move on with their lives, and I'm the one holding on to all of it.

When sunlight hits my face and I hear Nga shuffling out of our dorm room, all I want to do is sleep even more. Sleep away all these feelings and hope everything will resolve itself by the time I wake up again. But my phone vibrates and my heart drops, my mind racing at a hundred miles per hour thinking about Lan.

But it's not her. It's Dad. My heart drops for a second time. "Hi, Dad—"

"Oh good, you picked up." He sighs—which is a bad sign. Dad never sighs, and he sounds too relieved.

"Dad, what's wrong?"

"Your mom is in Sài Gòn. Like right now."

"*WHAT*? Why?"

"She . . . after the phone call with you, Mom booked the first plane ticket out of California to Sài Gòn that she could."

"I didn't think . . . what I said worked, that she'd literally take my advice. She's here to force me to come home, isn't she?"

Dad sighs again. "No, con, I don't think Mom's coming to bring you home. I think she's finally ready to come home herself."

My heart pounds. "What do I do? Do you know where she's going?"

"Go to her childhood home, con. This is her first time coming home. Welcome her back to her city. Show her what you love so much about Sài Gòn. Make her understand."

"Okay. Thanks, Dad." I hang up and text Cindy immediately.

Me: Cindy, I'm going to need you to do the biggest best friend favor I'll ever ask of you

Cindy: and that is . . . (also are you feeling better?)

Me: a bit. But um, any chance you can drive a motorbike?

Cindy: thank god for travel insurance, am I right? Jk, Nga can drive you (and I will track your location to make sure you're alive).

I breathe in and out, each breath getting shorter as we near Mom's childhood home. I look at the state of the house, it's the same as yesterday except duller. There's something melancholy about it now, something so sad that just looking at it makes me want to cry.

"You can do this," Cindy reassures me.

"Good luck, Vivi." Nga pats my back.

I only nod. I wonder if Mom knows that I'm here—would she be happy to see me?

I don't know if I can do this. I know I need to talk to Mom. I've never been surer in my life about anything else. But as I walk toward the house, my heart stops.

Mom.

Mom is in Việt Nam.

Standing in front of the house.

She's *here*.

"Mom?" I call out to her.

She whips her head back, and I prepare myself for anger—for Mom to yell at me and say that I'm awful and that she doesn't want me to come back with her and that—

Strong arms envelop me, pulling me into her embrace.

My voice cracks, releasing something high-pitched and a mixture between *I'm sorry* and *I missed you*. Mom doesn't speak at all. She just wraps me in her arms tightly and buries her head in the crook of my neck. She feels so small. All my anger and hurt dissipate and my arms find their way to her small, fragile back.

"Mommy nhớ con rất nhiều," she says, her voice squeaking as if she's been crying for a while.

I nod and hug her tighter. She smells like California, like a house that's overflowing with too much junk because my parents love to hoard. She smells like home. "I've missed you, too, Mom."

She releases me and touches my cheeks, studying every part of my face. "Con healthy and well. Mommy has been so worried."

I swallow. "Why are you outside?"

She sighs, her eyes looking at the house with sadness, and I realize that, like me, Mom probably feels scared—like she doesn't belong there anymore. "I . . . don't know how to face our family. I'm scared. Scared to see their faces when they look at me. Scared to know what they think of me."

I grab her hand, nudging us toward the door. "Mom, I'm here for you. This time, you're not alone."

She nods.

I knock, hearing muffled voices from the other side. Someone is shushing someone else. I knock again; this time the door clicks open, and Aunt Hiền's face comes into view.

I swallow. My throat is dry. I can feel Mom shaking, her grasp loosening as she takes in her sister's face.

"Hoa? Is that really you?" Aunt Hiền gapes at us, her eyes misty.

Mom lets go of my hand and runs toward Aunt Hiền, colliding into her sister's body as muffled sobs fill the air. "Chi Hiền. I've missed you so much."

"Hoa," Aunt Hiền cries. "I can't believe you're home. I can't believe you're back."

"I should have come back sooner. I should have been here for you when Má got sick. I did all that I could—all the money and medicine I can send—except actually be there for you."

Aunt Hiền shakes her head. "What matters is that you're here now. You're home."

As Mom and I stand outside Bà Ngoại's room, hand in hand, I think about how I never believed this moment would come—that one day, Mom and I would be in Việt Nam, visiting our family together. That one day, Mom would come back because of me.

Mom wipes her palm against her shirt, her shoulders visibly shaking.

"It'll be okay, Mom. I'm here."

We enter the dim room; the only sound is Bà Ngoại's breathing.

"Ma? I'm home," Mom whispers, her voice hoarse.

"Hoa oi, are you home?" Bà Ngoại calls out weakly. "Is that my Hoa? Did Hoa come back to me?"

Mom walks over to Bà Ngoại, still shaken, but her shoulders are higher, and she doesn't look as scared. "Ma, I'm sorry I just came back now. I'm sorry I . . . left you. I'm sorry I took so long."

Bà Ngoại chokes back a cry, her hand reaching for Mom. "Con, you don't have to say sorry. You don't have to say anything at all."

Mom sits next to Bà Ngoại's bed and holds her hand tightly, Bà Ngoại's chest rising up and down as she drifts off to sleep.

"Mom, không sao đâu. Bà Ngoại không sao đâu," I find myself telling her. *It's okay, Mom. Grandma's okay. We're okay.*

Aunt Hiền touches my shoulder and nods toward the corridor. "Go," she says.

Mom follows me outside, grabbing my arm and pulling me close. The walls don't feel as suffocating anymore. Fresh air greets us outside as the humidity hovers around us. I've been so used to this city's heat and humidity that I can't recall what California's dry heat feels like. Mom stares at the herb garden out front, carefully inspecting the leaves.

"I planted this."

Blinking, I imagine a younger version of Mom hunched over a pile of dirt, meticulously planting these herbs—the plants are still alive, too. "Oh. Wow."

Still inspecting the plants, she seems lost in her thoughts. I wonder what she's thinking about. So much has happened to her in the past forty-eight hours, and in this moment, I feel guilty for snapping back at her. Dusting herself off, she gets up and turns to me. "Vivi, come here."

I stiffen up immediately and do what she says.

The words spill out of me. "I'm sorry, Mom. I shouldn't have yelled at you like that. Or said all those awful things. I should have tried to understand you more."

"No." She shakes her head. "Mommy need to try to understand you more, con."

"I didn't want to disappoint you at all. I know that I shouldn't ask, because of the pain that it causes you, but I can't stop wondering about the past because it's a piece of my history, too."

She rubs her hands up and down my arms as if apologizing. "I know. I've hurt you very much, right?"

Tears well up again, and I can barely see her face in front of me. She tries wiping them from my cheeks, but I just let them fall. "Not as much as I probably hurt you."

Shaking her head, Mom embraces me again and lets my head rest on her shoulder this time. "It's been really hard for Mommy for a long time, con."

I squeeze her hand. "I want to hear, Mom. I'm ready. You can trust me."

This is the truth I've been waiting for.

She inhales sharply. "My relationship with your bà ngoại hasn't always been the best. We fought. A lot. She . . . has the tendency to scream."

I nod, recalling what Bà Ngoại had said to me when I visited her the first time—when Bà Ngoại screamed Mom's name.

"Your ông ngoại die early. Your grandpa was in the South Vietnamese Army and when he went to reeducation camp, he came back như người xa lạ. Like he wasn't my dad anymore."

My chest tightens as I imagine Grandpa returning home to our family, the horrors he witnessed and endured. The loss of the person he used to be because the war took it from him.

From all of us.

"It must have been so hard," I say, sniffling. "How did you leave?"

She sighs. "There was a boy."

My heart twists. I already know where this is going. "Was he your first love?" It's weird imagining Mom also in love in Việt Nam, falling for someone in this city under this very sky.

"He was. And I wanted to leave with him—look toward a place where I could find hope and survive. Hope because I'd find a job and send money back home. Hope that someday, I'd bring my mother and sister across the ocean, too. Your grandma begged me not to go—to not be so foolish and follow a boy to somewhere so far away from home. But I was so young, and so I ended up getting on that boat with the boy."

"What . . . happened to him?"

She gulped. "He left me the moment we got out of Việt Nam. Married another woman. It's shameful, isn't it? For me to leave everything I had here and follow him."

"Oh." So Mom was at sea and came to the United States all by herself. I can't imagine that, can't imagine all the trauma and hurt she had to endure. "I don't think it's shameful, Mom. You were young and lost, and yet you still kept going. And now I'm here, alive and in this world because of you."

I squeeze her, feeling her slumped shoulders against mine.

"To this day, I . . . I can sometimes see those memories in my nightmares—and the places I never want to revisit. I thought I could protect you by not bringing you here, by shielding you away from this country and everything that it has taken from me. But a lot of it was . . .

shame, too, shame that I left my family for a boy. Shame that I spent so many years alone in America, sleeping in a nail salon by myself."

I imagine a younger Mom running through this very yard, chasing her sister, and walking through the same roads that I have taken. Holding her tightly, I think about her on a small boat, confused and lost. I think about her alone in California, coming home with blisters and crying because she just wants to go home.

"Why didn't you tell me all of this? Why did you keep Việt Nam from me?"

She sighs. "Because to me, for a long time—and still now—Việt Nam has always been full of hurt, full of sadness. It was a dangerous place when I grew up, and I wanted to protect you. I know I should have told you a long, long time ago, should have let my sister and mother know about you—but after running away from home like that, I just didn't know how to tell them anything except wishing them well every time I wire them money. I was willing to live like that—to never come home again. Until you, con, pushed me to. I didn't know how much I've missed this city until I was home."

"Do you still feel the same, now that you're here? That everything is dangerous, and you want to leave again?"

She shakes her head. "No, only a little bit. This city has changed a lot. *I* have changed a lot. Even you, con, you've grown so much these past few months."

"I . . . really love Sài Gòn, Mom."

She nods. "I know, con, and you've always deserved to be here, to be with your family, and to know about Việt Nam."

Chapter Thirty-Three

LAN

Triết and Má insisted that I take the day off. This time, I listened to them. I do my usual morning routine: sweep the yard, water the orchids and herbs, and kiss Ba's picture on the altar. Then, instead of running out to the bánh mì stall, I make myself walk to the bakery. Ba's books have been there for too long. It's time I bring them home.

"Good morning, Lan!" Chú Hai calls when I open the door. "What brings you here today? Triết already picked up the baguettes this morning."

I clear my throat. "I'm here for the books."

He gives me a thumbs-up and disappears into the back, coming back with the box, which has been well cared for. "That's unusual. Is today a special day that I should know about?"

I smile at him. "I just felt like being brave today."

Not a lie. I'm still unsure if I'm ready to talk to Vivi again, but being brave also means taking one step at a time.

Waving goodbye to Chú Hai, I run toward the flimsy door and hike up to my favorite rooftop. The spot that used to be Ba's favorite, too.

Flipping open the first book from the box, I see Ba's handwriting scribbled across the top. *A masterpiece and must-read*, he wrote. I crack a smile. He annotated the entire book, writing down all his thoughts as he read. I flip through every page, carefully reading his annotations (*Brilliant! What an idea! Beautiful!*), brushing my fingers over his writing. Then, he wrote on the last page of the book, *To Lan, if you're ever bored and want some rainy day reads, this one's for you*. Laughing to myself, I clutch the book closer. Then I let the tears fall again.

I continue flipping through each book, tracing his thoughts and writing, and smiling to myself whenever I find my name.

Ba hoarded books because he wanted me to read them so he could hear my thoughts. I turn to the last page of the book in my hand and nearly cry again.

For when you grow up, he wrote.

As time passes and Sài Gòn comes alive, I stay where I am, reading through Ba's warm, loving words.

He'd write *for when you meet the love of your life* or *for when you don't know what to do*, as if he was afraid that he wouldn't be there for me when those things happened.

By the time that I'm finished, the sun has already gone to sleep. I breathe in the cool air, lie down, and stare at the bright sky. Tonight, Lyra and Orion join the Big and Little Dipper.

Ba, are you smiling at me from up there? I hope you are. I miss you so much. Please don't be upset that I took so long to come around. I promise I'll still take care of Má, but this time, I want to take care of myself, too.

I want to make you proud.

The North Star twinkles back at me as if hearing my wishes.

I'm drifting off to sleep when my phone rings next to me. "Hello?" I mumble.

Triết's voice comes through, although I hear Cindy in the background as well. "Hey, uh, are you by any chance with Vivi right now?"

My heart drops. "No, why? Did something happen to her?"

He sighs. "Cindy says that she dropped Vivi off at her mom's childhood home a while ago but she still hasn't come back to the dorm, and she's not responding to her texts, either. We're just worried."

I jump up, grab the box, and start running down the hill. "I'll find her. Don't worry."

"Are you sure? We can go together."

"It's okay. I'm coming back for my motorbike right now. I think that I should do this . . . alone."

I can feel Triết nodding. "I understand," he says. "I'll let Cindy know."

I race to the house, stumbling and scraping my knee against the wet concrete. I don't care. I keep going, looking at the twinkling North Star and praying that Vivi is safe. I haven't told her that I'm sorry yet. I haven't told her I *love* her yet.

As I near the house, Triết's already waiting outside with my motorbike. I give him the box, earning a confused look from him, and grab my helmet from his hand. Má's next to him, nodding her head and smiling at me. "I'm proud of you."

I maneuver through Sài Gòn's winding roads toward District 2. The night's brisk air beats on my back as I speed faster and faster, the wind muffling my ears while other motorbikes around me honk as I pass them. After twenty minutes, District 2 comes into view. Thank goodness that I've lived in this city all my life because I know all the alleyways by heart now. I recognize the church from last time and turn into the small alleyway next to it. A small two-story house with mismatched roofs comes into view. I hop off my motorbike, forgetting to turn it off, and run toward the door. Without a thought, I knock furiously. "Vivi!"

The small girl that's been the center of my world comes out. Her eyebrows scrunch when she meets my eyes. "Lan?"

Flustered, I look at my feet, unsure of how to handle this. The last time we talked, she had stomped out in anger. What can I say to make this all right again? What can I say to make her forgive me?

"I came to see you. I'm sorry."

"You hurt me, Lan." Her voice quivers. "I did everything I could to help you, and yet you pushed me away like I didn't mean anything to you. I didn't know if I'd see you again. If I'm going to leave Sài Gòn without ever talking to the girl I love."

My tears drip onto the pavement, each drop staining the concrete. "You're the reason I started writing again. The reason why I even got the courage to go grab my dad's books. Four years ago . . . my dad called me the day he felt sick, but I was out with friends and writing for the blog, so I didn't pick up. I blamed myself for everything that happened and was afraid to lose my mom in the same way. I know I've hurt you. I know I shouldn't have said everything that I did, and that all this time, all you've ever wanted was the best for me."

"It was always, always you, Vivi. You who pulled me out of my rut. You who made life in Sài Gòn so much more colorful. You who inspired my writing. You who helped me get this job. It has always been you."

She bites her lips, her chin trembling, and bursts into tears. "When I started this study abroad trip, I felt like an outsider. Like I was intruding and didn't belong in this city. Then, as I spent more time with you, I realized that maybe Sài Gòn is home. Maybe Sài Gòn is home because it's with you."

"I—"

Vivi shakes her head before continuing. "You were right, Lan. I don't understand how it feels. I am lucky, so lucky to have what I have. I'm so lucky to even be able to do this study abroad program and meet you. I'm so sorry I didn't think about how you'd feel. I don't know what it means to have to wake up before the sun even rises every day, to have to worry about where my food will come from next. I don't know how it feels to lose someone, or to carry the burden of being someone's livelihood. I'm sorry." Vivi kisses my forehead deeply, her lips brushing heat and warmth throughout my chest. "It has always been you for me, too."

"Vivi . . ." I can barely see her face through my tears and snot. She holds me closer and kisses my forehead, each touch igniting a fire inside of me.

"Today I finally went to grab the books that my dad has always wanted me to have. I was so scared to touch them because I didn't think that I was ever going to be ready. I held on to this promise that I made to him about protecting my mom forever because it gave me purpose. I was scared that I'd be lost by myself without him. It was an easy way out. You inspired me to be brave, and taught me that I can choose for myself," I choke out. "You are the best thing in my life. Sometimes I think about how my dad probably pulled some strings from wherever he is to get us together. And I don't want to lose you. Ever."

She looks at me, her eyes glossy. "Do you mean it?"

I nod. "Yeah. I do. I mean all of it. Everything I've said."

"What about the magazine contest—"

I inhale sharply, my heart beating fast as I prepare myself for what I'm about to tell her. This is it. This is my decision, and Vivi needs to know. "I'm going to take the journalism job with the magazine. Triết will step in for me—do whatever my mom needs. I . . . I'm finally going to do it, Vivi, finally going to see the cities outside of Sài Gòn."

"Lan." She chokes out a sob. "I'm so proud of you. You are so talented and you deserve this so much and no one works harder than you and no one is as creative, as masterful with their writing, and no one can ever compare to you—and I hope you know that. I love you."

My heart swells. "I love you, too," I whisper before leaning in, the air sizzling between us just before her lips meet mine. We embrace each other tightly, tenderly, and as if our bodies are so delicate we might break. I lean in deeper, caressing her face with my hands. Warmth spreads through my body, and I nudge my mouth with everything I've got—all my sorrys, my desperation, and my overwhelming feelings for her.

"I love you, too, Lan," she says, her face flushed between my palms.

Someone clears their throat behind us. "Vivi? Is this Lan?"

We jump from our position and untangle our limbs from each other. Vivi, red from head to toe, manages to squeak—not speak. "Yes, Mom."

I gape at her. Her *mom*? I must have missed a chapter. Or two. "Chào cô, I'm Lan. I'm Vivi's, uh." I give Vivi a side glance.

"Girlfriend. Yes, this is my girlfriend," she says, and grabs me to straighten my back.

Her mom softens her gaze at us and takes my head in her hands. "Con, thank you for taking care of Vivi for me. She loves Sài Gòn, and I think you're the reason why."

I blush. "It was nothing, I didn't mind it at all."

She nods to Vivi and me before speaking the phrase that all Vietnamese mothers use interchangeably with *I love you*. "Have you eaten?"

Acknowledgments

Thank you for reading Lan and Vivi's story! It's still surreal to me that this book is out—that a sapphic rom-com featuring two Vietnamese characters set in my home city exists in the world. So thank you, readers, for picking up this little book of mine.

Thank you to my incredible agent, Naomi Davis. I am so lucky to know you, to work with you, and to be championed by you. I still remember the very day when the stars aligned, and your email landed in my inbox during my college lecture asking if we could set up a call. That day was my canon event and irreversibly changed my life—YOU changed my life! Your unwavering support, wisdom, and love were my beacons of light throughout this journey, and I cannot wait to see what other beautiful things we'll build together.

Thank you to Dana Chidiac and Valery Badio; what a dream it is to work with the most brilliant people! Thank you, both, for seeing the heart of the story when it was a Hot Mess and thank you for all the love you've poured into *A Bánh Mì for Two*. Without your vision and encouragement (especially laughing at my attempts to crack jokes in the comments), this book and I wouldn't be where we are today. Thank you.

To the entire team at Henry Holt Books for Young Readers and everyone who worked tirelessly behind the scenes and made my dream come true, especially Ann Marie Wong, Jean Feiwel, Alexei Esikoff, Jie Yang, and everyone in sales, marketing, and publicity. A million thank-yous will not suffice. Many thanks to Molly Murakami, Abby Granata, and Aurora Parlagreco for the cover—I'm so lucky to work with such talented people. Special thanks to Anh-Thu Nguyen for being the best authenticity reader and the best bánh mì partner a gal could ask for, I look forward to venturing to Bánh Mì Huynh Hoa with you in HCMC again soon!

To everyone who has blurbed this book and gave *A Bánh Mì for Two* your love and support, thank you thank you thank you!

To my family: Bố, Mẹ, and Trâm. Our family history and life in Sài Gòn greatly inspired this book, but so did our chaotic and loving family. Everything I've learned about love I've learned it from you. To my extended family in Việt Nam, especially my grandparents and aunts, thank you for always taking me on motorbike rides around Sài Gòn and stuffing me with bánh mìs until I'm full.

To the writers and friends who believe in me tenfold more than I've ever believed in myself. Wen-yi Lee, I truly think all the cosmic forces and invisible strings tied us together! What a whirlwind of a journey it has been for us, from pondering if we'd ever get published while riding the LA Metro to us both accepting our debut offers the same week . . . and now debuting two weeks apart. From Singapore to LA, I'm thankful our transpacific friendship. You're forever the *Reputation* album to my *Lover* album, the beautiful horror author to my silly rom-com author, and my person to run to amidst all the highs and lows of publishing.

To the friend who has been there since *A Bánh Mì for Two*'s birth and can pinpoint the book's origin story, Victoria Russo, I can never thank you enough (and I owe you my life, for all the encouragements you've showered me with when I didn't know how to outline a novel, let alone write one). To Manasa Uppili, Divine (and for being the actual Vivi to my Vivi in the book), Delphine, and Cossette, I'm so happy the internet managed to forge me such wonderfully deep friendships. To the writing and author friends that shared wisdom, tears, joys, and jokes with me: Clare Osongco, Gayle Gaviola, Lilly Lu, Ann Zhao, Hien Nguyen, Busayo Matuluko, Brandon Hoang, Julie Tieu, Hannah Sawyer, Kiana Krystle, Aislynn Clavido, Janetsa Keo, Mia, Selena, Elise, Tiff. Thank you to the Avengers of Color Mentorship program and the 2021 cohort—what a group of extraordinary writers! I cannot wait to feature all our books side by side on my bookshelf. To the Gen Zs in publishing, for being there for me as we all navigate this journey together, holding hands and blindly stumbling our way through. To friends who know next to nothing about publishing but scream about it with me anyway: Daisy Frias, Donny Vuong, Emily Ly, Thang Ton, Ken Nguyen, Lee Matthews, Seth Sherwood, Anna Phommachanthone, Amanda Leonard, Kamakshi Shah, Sam Tran, and so many more.

To my fairy godmothers Carolyn Huỳnh, Amanda Khong, Viviann Do, and Jes Vũ, Los Angeles would be so lonely without you all. Every day I look forward to the unhinged chaos that would inevitably unfold because we are messy, messy Vietnamese women. I am eternally grateful for all your love (and, of course, car rides with me as the passenger princess throughout SoCal).

Thank you to all the Vietnamese and Vietnamese diaspora writers who came before me, who wrote and fought so I could tell my own stories. Special thanks to Michelle Quach, Loan Le, Nguyen Phan Que Mai, Vanessa Le, Hanh Bui, and Trang Thanh Tran, for lending me your support, for reading, and for your friendship.

To everyone I've met at Franklin & Marshall College, especially the Writers House and the Asian American Alliance: for fostering my love for community, the Asian diaspora identity, and creative writing.

To my cats, Obi Nguyen and Boba Nguyen. My little menaces who snuggled me warm as I wrote and rewrote this book.

To Jon Burkhardt, for feeding me smiley-face avocado toasts, heart-shaped pizzas, and perfectly cut fruits (just like my Vietnamese mother) as I chip away at my manuscripts. For grounding me when life sometimes slips beneath my feet, and for listening to the strange stories in my head even when you have no clue what I'm rambling on and on about. You are my biggest cheerleader. I adore you and I can't wait to celebrate many, many more book launches together.

To you, readers, and especially queer Asian readers, for championing this book just by picking it up. For championing two Vietnamese girls softly falling in love. Thank you, with all my heart.